Listening for Lions

Listening
for Lions

GLORIA WHELAN

HARPERCOLLINS*PUBLISHERS*

Library of Congress Cataloging-in-Publication Data
Whelan, Gloria.

Listening for lions / Gloria Whelan.

p.   cm.

Summary: Left an orphan after the influenza epidemic in
British East Africa in 1919, thirteen-year-old Rachel is
tricked into assuming a deceased neighbor's identity to
travel to England, where her only dream is to return to
Africa and rebuild her parents' mission hospital.

ISBN: 0-06-058174-3 — 0-06-058175-1 (lib. bdg.)

[1. Self-realization—Fiction.   2. Africa, East—History—
20th century—Fiction.   3. Orphans—Fiction.
4. Physicians—Fiction.   5. Great Britain—History—
George V, 1910–1936—Fiction.]   I. Title.

PZ7.W5718Li 2005   2004020844
[Fic]—dc22   CIP
                                                   AC

Typography by Amy Ryan
1 2 3 4 5 6 7 8 9 10
❖
First Edition

To
Joe and Linda
Jenny and Mike

CONTENTS

Listening for Lions

BOOK ONE

Rachel Sheridan

ONE

*I*t crept up on us like the hyenas I heard at night from my window, drawn to us, Kanoro said, by the smell of death. It was 1919, and because the Great War was over, we had thought all the deaths were at an end, but it wasn't so. All over the world the cruel influenza had been taking lives. In America half a million people died; in India, many, many millions. In British East Africa, where I was living, the influenza began in the seaport of Mombasa, traveled three hundred miles to the city of Nairobi, and from there crept onto the farms and plantations and into the Kikuyu and Masai *shambas*. At last it reached Tumaini, the mission hospital where my father was a doctor and my mother a teacher. The influenza killed my parents.

My parents had been sent from England as missionaries to the Kikuyu and the Masai. There had been a minister at our mission, but he had left to serve in the war. Father had tried to carry on with the church work, but he was often too busy with the hospital. He said, "When a man lies with his leg sliced open and the bone sticking out, there is no time for preaching." My parents had been in Africa for fourteen years. I was born the year after they arrived. Africa was the only home I knew. I could not imagine living anywhere else.

The beds in our hospital were filled with Africans and the wards and hallways crowded with their families. Father treated sleeping sickness, plague, smallpox, and leprosy. He helped mothers whose babies had a hard time being born. One miracle especially filled me with joy. I watched as blind people were led to the hospital. When Father removed their cataracts, they walked home on their own. I would close my eyes and imagine I could not see. After a minute of darkness I would open my eyes to the sun and all the bright colors that were Africa. Later, when I had to live in England's bleak winters, I wished for my own miracle to give me back Africa's brightness.

The families of the patients who came to our hospital camped out on the grounds of the hospital, for they would not leave the care of a family member to a stranger. All day long you could hear the Kikuyu chattering to one another and smell the smoke of their fires as they roasted a goat or cooked their maize porridge, *posho*. The men of the Masai wore togalike cloths draped over their shoulders and carried spears. The men of the Kikuyu wore blankets or sometimes nothing at all. The Kikuyu women were clothed in leather aprons or hundreds of strings of bright beads. When the Kikuyu came to work at the hospital as nurses and assistants, the men wore khaki shorts and shirts and the women plain white dresses and caps. They were like birds who had shed their rich plumage.

Father had begged the mission board in England for another doctor and a nurse, but the war had taken all the doctors and nurses, so Father trained the Kikuyu to assist him. One of the men, Ita, was already performing minor surgery, and one of the nurses, Wanja, was the anesthetist.

The Masai would not be trained and seldom came to our church. The Kikuyu first came out of respect for Father, but soon they were enjoying the singing and many eagerly took up the new faith. Mother had taught me to play hymns on the piano, and the Kikuyu would call out their favorites and I would turn the pages of the hymnal to their choices, until after a while I knew them all by heart and could play as loudly as they could sing.

We were only a small hospital. There was a large hospital in Nairobi for white people and another for the native Africans, but the city was a long drive over bad roads. When I went into Nairobi with my parents to McKinnon's store, it was by oxcart. My favorite place in Nairobi was the Indian bazaar, with its wonderful smells and its counters heaped with spices. My parents didn't mix with the wealthy English planters and would not have been welcome in their cricket and tennis clubs. "With their drinking and foolery," my father said, "they are like the people of Sodom and Gomorrah. They are headed for destruction."

On the very few occasions I had been allowed to accompany Mother and Father to Nairobi, the planters we saw going about on the streets appeared well behaved. I supposed the middle of the day was not the time for drinking and foolery.

One of the farmers I disliked, a Mr. Pritchard, had a sisal plantation near our hospital. Occasionally he sent over one of the natives on his plantation who had taken ill, but he would never inquire as to how the man was doing. Once a Kikuyu who worked for him had been brought to the hospital by the other workers because he had been beaten by Mr. Pritchard. He was covered with blood, and his ribs were broken. It was the only time I heard Father use a curse word. Mother and Father did not gossip, but on that evening Father spoke again of drinking and foolery. I heard him say, "Pritchard is sure to gamble away that farm in one of his drinking bouts."

During the war many of the Kikuyu had been drafted by the British to serve as porters in the British army. British soldiers had fought the Germans in nearby German East Africa. After the war the Kikuyu came back with nothing but bits of their worn uniforms, but they had seen a world beyond the native reserves. They no longer wanted anything to do with men like Mr. Pritchard, but they had to pay hut taxes to the British government, and the only way the Kikuyu could get the money for the taxes was to work for the planters.

The Pritchards had a daughter, who, like me, had ginger hair. Because they had not often seen red hair, the Kikuyu were sure it was a kind of sickness and did not understand why my parents could not cure me. The Pritchards' daughter was my age but better fed, like a plump wood pigeon. Her dresses were silk and her hair was tied with a matching silk ribbon. I stared at her when our oxcart took us past her plantation, but she never noticed me.

Although I looked forward to the excitement of a visit to Nairobi, there was more than enough to amuse me in the African countryside. When I was little, Kanoro kept track of me because my parents were occupied. He warned me of the anthills and snatched me away from the mambas and puff adders and the little African garter snakes that looked so pretty and were deadly. When I came indoors, he made me hunt for ticks on my legs and showed me how to squash them with my fingernails. He was so clever with a needle that he could dig a chigger from under my toenail without my feeling it. He warned me about falling into the holes made by antbears. He would not let me run about in the evenings when the leopards were rumored to be in the nearby bush. Leopards, Kanoro said, were the only animal that killed not for food, but for the pleasure of killing.

Kanoro showed me how to find wild honey and taught me the difference between the various kinds of weaverbird nests: the long nests that hung like bells, the neat nests and the messy ones, and the nests with many entrance holes where several weaverbirds lived sociably together.

Kanoro always said just what he thought. This was a great relief to me, for before they turned their scolding into words, my parents took a long time to think over something foolish or disobedient I had done. All the time I was waiting for their words, I was worrying about what they were going to say. Kanoro just said that I was a stupid girl or a bad one. I learned to go to him if I was worried about something. His broad forehead would pleat into wrinkles, and pronouncing the Swahili word for difficulties, *wasiwasi*, he would find a way out of my troubles.

As I grew older, Kanoro trusted me with my freedom, and after the morning lessons Mother had set me the night before, I did as I liked. I chased the little dassies, the smallest of the antelopes, and fed the monkeys until they became such a nuisance that the feeding was forbidden. I played among the Kikuyu herds of goats, choosing one of the long-legged kids to carry about with me. I sat by our small pond and winced as the wood stork speared a frog with its sharp bill. I lay in the hammock watching the hawks overhead and breathed in the fragrance of the cedar and the sharp smell of eucalyptus. Sometimes in the distance I saw vultures circling, and I wondered if a lion had caught a zebra or cut an impala from the herd. Though I loved the lions, and thrilled when I heard their roars in the night, I would be sorry for the zebra or the impala. On hot days I would look at Mount Kenya lording it over the plains and imagine the coolness of the snow that lay on the mountain. I wondered what it would feel like to have snow fall from the heavens upon me, for my parents had told me that in England such a thing happened. It never occurred to me that one day it would happen to me.

I was welcome in the *shambas*, the small farms, of the Kikuyu, who sometimes begged for locks of my hair, which I believe they used as a charm against evil. In return they would cut a length of sugarcane for me with their sharp *pangas*. Their huts were made of straw and looked like half-opened parasols. There was not much to see inside the huts, only a pot or two and a few drinking gourds and perhaps a wooden bench. Outside the huts the women with their long wooden pestles pounded maize for *posho*. All hours of the day I heard the pounding as regular as my breathing. When I went home, the smoke from their cooking fires clung to my clothes.

The Kikuyu were great storytellers. I had grown up with the Kikuyu and spoke Swahili, and I sat quietly and listened while they told one another stories of their achievements in war or in the trading of goats. In that way their children learned of past times. This telling of tales always seemed to me a much more interesting way of keeping stories alive than the history books that I had to study. I forgot what was in the books, but I remembered the stories.

The Sunday after I turned twelve, Father told me to listen closely to his sermon. He chose as his text the verses in Ephesians in which St. Paul admonishes us to follow the Lord in good works. Father said that now each day after my lessons were over, I could no longer do just as I liked. I was to spend time in the hospital being useful. I didn't like the hospital, with its smell of disinfectant and all its misery, and asked why Father had not chosen as his text the part in Ephesians where St. Paul says by grace are ye saved and not by works. Father said I was being pert.

The Kikuyu nurse Jata taught me how to take temperatures and pulses. She showed me how to coax the patients into taking their medicine, which they often refused, and how to give them goat broth with a lot of salt to treat the dehydration that came with cholera. It was especially difficult to watch over the Masai patients, who were so tall and regal herding their cattle but who collapsed when they had to be hospitalized. They would not let you do anything for them, hating to be dependent. They could not even stand to be inside a building, and it was said that if they were put into prison, they died.

I scrubbed the operating room, which I hated to do because there was blood and because I never got it clean enough for Jata, who was a hard taskmaster and accepted no excuses. I saw that the relatives had maize for their porridge and that their fires did not burn out of control. I reported arguments that got out of hand, for the Kikuyu and the Masai were not always friendly to one another. I watched over patients to be sure they ate nothing before their surgery, for the families wanted to feed them up so that they would be strong for "the cutting." I washed the flies from the corners of the eyes of the *mtotos*, the little children who hung about the hospital.

At first, like the Masai, I could not stand being shut up all afternoon inside the hospital. I would sneak out whenever I could, though I knew that Father would scold me and Mother would look very sad at my sins. After a while the hospital was not so bad. By the end of my first year I could wrap a bandage around an injury and calm the fears of relatives who were sure the hospital meant certain death. When Kanoro's son, Ngigi, stepped on broken glass and his foot became infected and might have to be taken off, I spent all my time cleansing and bandaging the foot. I tried to cheer the restless *mtoto* by bringing him bits of the outdoors: a rare purple butterfly in a jar, an abandoned bird's nest cleverly woven, a new lamb from his father's flock to hold in his arms. When there was no taking off his foot and the bandages were removed and he walked again, I began to think my hours in the hospital were not wasted.

There were things I avoided. I hurried away when the

lepers came for treatment, with their fingerless hands and their faces without noses. Yet when Father sent me to one of the Kikuyu *shambas* to remind an old woman to come for her treatment, I marveled at how cleverly she was weaving a basket with only a few fingers. When she offered to teach me, I crept closer to her, and in no time I had forgotten she was a leper.

I was proud that Father allowed me to help him, but it was from Mother that I learned softness and understanding. When she was finished with her teaching, Mother helped out at the hospital. Father would not break a rule, but Mother cared nothing for a rule when someone at the hospital suffered under that rule. Mother and Father disagreed over the enforcement or the breaking of such rules. They were both stubborn, and there would be a day of uncomfortable silence when the hospital staff would roll their eyes at one another and keep out of Father's path, but Mother usually got her way. Father might turn away from our church services a man who had two wives. Mother would point out that it took one wife to pound maize all day for the family's porridge and another one to tend to the crops and the children. The man would be allowed to join the congregation, but Father insisted there must be no third wife. I came to understand that though there were arguments, Father depended on Mother's tender heart and Mother relied on Father's rules.

When Mother came home tired from the teaching and

the hospital, I would rub her back and bring her a cup of tea. Then she might tell me stories of how she and Father had met in England in the church orphanage where they had both grown up. The orphanage had been very strict. The girls lived in one building and the boys in another, and they saw one another only at morning and evening Sunday church services. They were given lumpy porridge to eat and bread without butter. The orphans had to listen to someone reading from the Bible or some other edifying book during meals and could not talk with one another. If they disobeyed, the boys were beaten and the girls were shut into their room and fed on bread and water. They were not allowed to have a special friend and were given cast-offs from parishioners to wear. Mother said she would see a dress on a parish girl many times before it was given to her. Once, Mother said, she had worn such a dress and had to endure the girl's giggles when she recognized her dress on Mother.

The boys and girls were taught their lessons in separate schools. Father did very well and thanks to a kind bene-factor was sent to university to study to become a doctor for the missions. When Father was ready to leave for the missions, he was told it would be better if he had a wife to help him. A meeting was arranged with Mother, who had stayed on in the orphanage to teach little children at the orphanage school. On a Sunday afternoon they were invited to take tea together at the vicar's home.

"It was a small miracle," Mother said. "In five minutes I knew I liked your father, but I thought it immodest to appear eager, so I insisted on two more teas at the vicar's."

"I had to sit there in a stiff collar," Father said, "talking nonsense. I have heard how in the times of chivalry men had to joust with sharp lances for their women, but I don't believe they ever had to eat so many of the vicar's wife's biscuits. Like rocks they were."

Because the church had seen to Father's training, he was expected to serve the church in the mission field, but that was no hardship for Mother and Father. "We had no family in England," Mother said, "and it's a cold country. Here the sun shines and all the Kikuyu are our family. Someday, I suppose, we must all return to England, but I hope the day will not come soon."

For Mother and Father the day never came.

TWO

*I*t was a hot afternoon in January. I was sitting on the hospital steps ripping a width of cloth into bandages and longing for the cool of the evening. A Kikuyu man was brought to the hospital by his family. I could see the small party coming across the dry plain from a long way away. There had been a drought, and a train of little puffs of red dust followed along behind them and settled like a powdery rain on the leaves of the acacia trees. After depositing the homemade stretcher and its burden in the hospital, the family stood about peering into the hospital windows, waiting for some word about the patient.

After Father examined the man, there was an unusual bustle of activity in the hospital. Father sent me to get Mother. Quickly a contagious ward was created by stringing a curtain across a doorway. I recognized the curtain, for it had hung between rooms in our house and I had helped Mother in the hemming of it.

Father and Mother whispered together and then told me that I must go home and stay away from the hospital.

When I asked why, Father said, "It's influenza, Rachel, and it's extremely contagious."

"But what about you and Mother?"

"We'll take precautions."

"Why can't I take precautions?" I was excited at the thought of this exotic and dangerous disease appearing at our own hospital there on the plains of Africa. I didn't want to be left out.

"Don't argue with me, Rachel." It was Father's God-to-Moses voice, and I said no more.

Mother put her arm around me. "Rachel, if the influenza spreads, your father and I are going to have all we can manage. We don't want to be distracted by worrying about you. And stay away from the Kikuyu *shambas*. We don't know how quickly the influenza will spread." Reluctantly I left the hospital.

I had heard that in Nairobi there were cases of influenza in both the native hospital and the hospital for whites. Letters from the mission house in England and the local newspaper were full of frightening reports of the illness sweeping the world. But like the war that had ended in November, it was something that was happening far away. It had not been real. Now it was real.

As I left the hospital, I looked out across the plains that

spread mile upon mile to the ridges of the distant hills. There was a verse in Revelations that always frightened me: "And I looked, and behold a pale horse: and his name that sat on him was Death, and Hell followed with him." I saw the pale horse and its rider galloping across those plains and finding us.

Kanoro kept a ladder against the house so that he could reach the roof for easy patching when heavy rains found their way through our ceiling. The roof was nothing more than sheets of corrugated iron with heavy stones to keep the sheets in place. When I was younger, I was often on the roof for a better view of the plains. Now I climbed up the ladder and looked out into the distance. There was no pale horse, only a herd of zebras far away, their black stripes against their white hides like writing, like an urgent message that was impossible to make out. In the distance I saw a small group of Kikuyu bringing another stretcher.

Kanoro came to tell me that Mother and Father wouldn't be home for their noon meal. "The man they brought in this morning, he died," Kanoro said. "Now there are three more in the hospital; one of them is a Masai. The Masai was so sick, he made no protest at going into the hospital. Your mother said you are to take her class of little ones," he said. Kanoro hurried away, trying to hide his worry from me, but I knew him too well.

There were no books in Swahili except for the Bible and a hymnal, so I read to the small children from *Alice's*

Adventures in Wonderland, translating from English to Swahili as I went. I had them all practice smiling like the Cheshire Cat and taught them the "Twinkle, Twinkle, Little *Popo*" poem.

After class I curled up in a hammock strung between two cedar trees with a dog-eared copy of Dickens's *David Copperfield.* I had few books, and those I had were worn, with bits of their pages nibbled by beetles who loved the books as much as I did. David's miserable childhood in London, his cruel schoolmaster, and his horrible job in the blacking factory reminded me of my own parents' youth in an orphanage. It didn't occur to me at that moment that I, too, might become an orphan. I think I believed that because Father was a doctor, he would let no illness come to our family. Instead, I worried about Kanoro and his family and all the Kikuyu whose *shamba*s I had visited. I had played with their children and sat beside them in our church. I feared for them and could not keep my mind on my book.

Several times I walked to the hospital and thought of disobeying Father by going inside, but seeing the crowd of families gathered in little worried clusters, I turned back. I wasn't hungry, and at dinnertime I only nibbled on a chicken leg and a bit of goat cheese.

I couldn't sleep and kept a lantern on against the dark-ness. When it got too hot, I went out onto the porch and listened to the crickets and the cicadas, the crickets' chirp measured and regular, the cicadas with their frantic shrieks, sounding more like I felt. Later I heard the growls of a lion, faint and coming from a distance. It was a familiar sound and almost comforting, for I thought of the lions as soldiers of the night, patrolling all the dark places.

It was midnight before Mother came home. Her shoulders sagged and her dress was wrinkled and soiled. Her hair straggled out of its neat bun. I hurried to heat some water so she could wash.

Mother explained, "Your father is staying at the hospital to ready it for a large number of cases. Rachel, your father will sleep in the hospital for a few days until the worst of this is over. You are not to worry, and you are not to come to the hospital. The classes will not be meeting—the children in a group might spread the flu. Kanoro will let you know what is happening. And Rachel, you must pray that our people will be spared."

I went to my room without my usual good-night kiss, for Mother was keeping her distance from me. I was awake most of the night, persecuted by a yellow house bat that had found its way into my room and was ricocheting from wall to wall. Ordinarily I would have called Mother, but I didn't want to awaken her. At last I got up my courage, and seizing a broom, I swiped at the bat until it fell to the floor quite dead. It was that night that I first heard the hyenas.

Each day brought more influenza victims to the hospital. The Masai and Kikuyu families crowded about the hospital grounds. Because of the contagion they were not allowed to care for their families in the hospital. Jata took sick, but in a few days she was back at work. Rumors about the influenza spread as quickly as the disease. We heard that the hospitals in Nairobi were so crowded, they were not accepting patients. A steady stream of patients was carried to our hospital, and many were carried away with grieving and wailing.

Kanoro was helping in the hospital. Left to myself all day with nothing to do but worry, I was glad to take over the feeding and milking of our goats and the tending of our garden. When she had first come to Africa, Mother had tried to plant English flowers—daffodils, primroses, and wallflowers. In the unforgiving dry earth and hot sun they wilted and crisped and gave up. Now our garden held practical things: sweet potatoes and corn, the same things the Kikuyu grew in their gardens.

I would hoe a row or two and then forget about my work, standing and looking at the hospital, listening to a hoopoe bird in the distance, wondering what was happening. It seemed unfair to me that everyone else was fighting the epidemic and I could do nothing. I argued with Mother each evening when she returned home, but she wouldn't change her mind. After a while I saw how tired she was, and I took pity on her and ceased my pleading.

Kanoro's son, Ngigi, brought me the news from the Kikuyu *shambas*, which were nearly deserted. The Kikuyu men were moving far away from the illness, accompanied by the women carrying their babies on their backs, their little ones skipping along beside them. Their goats and sheep went with them, but their crops, left behind, went untended, so hunger would go with them as well.

On Sunday neither Father nor Mother left the hospital to come to church. This was more alarming to me than the illness itself. It was Sunday, and there must be church. I put on my one good dress and squeezed into my patent leather shoes. Trembling at my audacity, I stood at the pulpit where Father always stood. Only Kanoro and Ngigi and another Kikuyu whom I did not recognize came to the church. I read the fortieth Psalm, which always frightened me at first and then made me feel better, "He brought me up also out of an horrible pit, out of the miry clay, and set my feet upon a rock, and established my goings." I then went to our old piano, chased away a mouse that was nesting there, and played "Angels! Ever bright and fair," which the four of us sang in wavering voices. After that Kanoro and Ngigi and the other Kikuyu left the church and I trailed after them, not sure that God had bothered with my poor attempt.

Kanoro was waiting for me. "It is bad at the hospital," he said. He looked at me strangely and then in a half whisper added, "The *memsahib* is not well."

In church the heat had made my dress cling wetly to my back; now I felt cold all over. "What's wrong with Mother?"

Kanoro only shook his head and walked off in the direction of the hospital. I ran after him and grabbed at his arm. "Kanoro, does Mother have influenza?"

"It is better you talk to your father." He would say nothing more, only swatting at his face as if to get rid of an insect, but it was tears that he was chasing away.

In the distance I saw a family bearing away a stretcher, the sounds of their wails like the mournful cries of the wood pigeons. Though the hospital had been forbidden to me, I pushed through the entrance, making my way through the crowds of Kikuyu and Masai waiting for news of their relatives. The wards were crowded. There were twice as many beds as usual. I had only just walked into the hospital when I came upon my father.

His eyes were red, and his face bristled with a beard of several days' growth. He stared at me and there was no welcome in his eyes. He asked in a gruff voice, "Rachel, what are you doing here?"

I had expected an angry scolding for going against his orders, but the question was asked in a hopeless way, as if he carried a great basket of questions and was weary of the asking of them.

"I wanted to see Momma," I said, using the name I had called her when I was little.

"I am afraid you are too late. Your dear mother has just passed away. I was coming to the house to tell you. It's a sad day for us." Father was not an affectionate man. I never held it against him, for I thought that when he was a child, there had been no one to teach him affection. Now he surprised me by putting an arm around me and holding me tightly. After a moment he drew away. "This won't do, Rachel. I and everyone in this hospital will be a danger to you. You must go back to the house. I'll be there soon. The burial will be today. I will leave it to you to select a place in the churchyard, and Kanoro must prepare it." His voice wavered. "You must ask the Lord for strength to bear this." He turned abruptly away from me and vanished into one of the wards.

I left the hospital and made my way toward the churchyard, passing our goat pen. One of the kids was nuzzling its mother, wanting to nurse. Once I had had to bottle-feed a young kid that had lost its mother. If we had not fed it, it would have died. How old, I wondered, must a child be to survive after its mother has died? I knew that I would survive, but I was not sure of the way it was to be done.

Not many girls must choose the place where their mother's coffin is to lie. The churchyard was small, with only two wooden crosses to mark the graves of Kanoro's father and a missionary preacher who had come long before us. The grasses had been scythed, and a few flat-topped acacia trees made loose circles of shade. Kanoro, who stood beside me with a shovel and with tears streaming down his face, must have wondered at my dry eyes, but I had turned myself to stone for my task.

I chose a small plot that looked out at the hills, remembering Mother marveling at how the hills were blue and misty in the morning, purple and shimmering in the late afternoon, and then at nightfall nothing more than a deeper darkness in the distance.

I could not bear to see Kanoro at his work, but went to gather flowers for Mother. I returned with a bouquet of the flowers that grow wild in the bush, spikey blue thistles and red and yellow aloes. I thought them too garish for their sad purpose and wished I had the soft English flowers Mother longed for. Father was already there, and beside him were men carrying Mother's coffin. Father had shaved his beard and wore his black suit. He took my hand and drew me to him. His hand felt hot in mine, and he wiped beads of sweat from his forehead. Kanoro and Jata, the nurse who had been especially close to Mother, stood beside us. The others could not leave their work at the hospital.

Father began to read the burial service. His voice, usually so strong, wavered as he read, "I will lift up mine eyes unto the hills, from whence cometh my help." He was thinking, as I had, of Mother's love for the hills. Father was unsteady on his feet, and once Kanoro reached out to support him. I bit my lip to keep from crying, imagining that Mother was watching us and would be proud of me.

As Father closed his Bible and the coffin was lowered into the ground, a large black car drove up to the hospital.

It was so rare to see a car that the owner of each car was known. This was the Pritchards' car. I had seen it once in Nairobi, with Mrs. Pritchard and her daughter riding in the back. I had stood and stared at them, thinking what a treat it would be to ride around in such a car instead of the dusty, slow-moving oxcart that carried us. All the car doors opened at once, and Mr. Pritchard was hurrying toward us, his wife beside him, his daughter lying in his arms.

Mr. Pritchard was panting a little from the running and the weight of his daughter. "Valerie is very ill," he said to Father. "There was no time to take her into Nairobi." The girl's eyelids fluttered and she made a small moaning sound. All her plumpness was gone. Her face was tinged with blue, and there were brownish spots on her cheeks.

Father accompanied the Pritchards to the hospital and I followed along, reluctant to be alone after all the sadness. In spite of my misery, I was fascinated with the drama of the car and the sick girl cradled in her father's arms, the father in his white linen suit and the mother in a blue linen dress and a large straw hat trimmed with silk flowers. It was like a story that you might find in some book, except that all the people were real and their worry the most real thing of all.

As we reached the hospital, Mr. Pritchard said, "You must clear the natives out of a ward for her."

"That's impossible," Father said. "Even if I would agree to such a thing, we are overcrowded and there would be no place for our patients to go."

"I will not have her in a bed next to some filthy native."

They were at the hospital entrance. Father stood in front of the door, barring their entrance. "If your daughter becomes a patient in the hospital, I shall do all I can for her, just as I do for any patient who comes to my hospital, but it is my hospital and I will make the rules. If you don't like that, you may take her elsewhere."

I thought Mr. Pritchard was going to strike Father. His wife put her hand on his arm. "Aldon, please do as the doctor says."

Father lifted the girl from Mr. Pritchard's arms, and I saw Father look at her ginger hair, so much like mine. His face softened and I knew he was thinking that it might have been me, sick and helpless, in his arms. He handed her gently to Jata.

The Pritchards tried to follow them into the hospital, but Father put a hand on either side of the entrance like Solomon holding up the pillars of the temple. "I can't allow you to come in. The whole hospital is a contagion ward. It's for your own good."

"I don't think you understand what we feel," Mr. Pritchard said. "Suppose it were a member of your family."

Father gave him a steely look. "I have just buried my wife."

Mrs. Pritchard said, "Surely you understand that we cannot leave our child."

Father said, "You may wait in my home. Rachel will see to your comfort. Now I must take care of your daughter."

The Pritchards looked at me with surprise. It was the first time they had noticed me. As we walked toward the house, Mrs. Pritchard said, "We are very sorry for your loss." Her voice had an unpleasant shrillness to it, like the sharp cries of the cicadas. She walked ahead of me and into the house without waiting for me to invite her inside. Mr. Pritchard brushed me aside as well, so I was the last to enter my own home.

Looking about him, Mr. Pritchard demanded, "Is this your only house?"

"Yes." I wondered if he thought I was hiding our real house to mislead him.

Mrs. Pritchard wiped the seat of a chair with a lace handkerchief and sat down. Mother was a conscientious housekeeper, but Mother had not been in the house for several days and dust had blown through the open windows.

"Where is your servant?" Mr. Pritchard asked. "Perhaps he could bring my wife some tea."

We had no servants, only Kanoro to help us. "I'll get some tea," I said. I was glad for a task that would take me away from them. I wanted only to be by myself and grieve for my mother. In the kitchen I emptied some water from a bottle into the kettle and set it to boil. I put some milk in a pitcher. A tear fell into the pitcher, and I recalled a children's book in which a child's tears curdled the milk. I didn't like the Pritchards and hoped my tear would sour their milk. Reluctantly I opened our last packet of sweet biscuits and arranged them neatly on a plate. When the tea was ready, I took the tray into the sitting room and placed it on our table.

Mrs. Pritchard sipped the tea but refused the biscuits. She blinked away tears. "Valerie is our only child," she said. "She was going to visit her grandfather in England."

My dislike disappeared. I only felt sorry for her. I tried to think of something comforting to say. "You mustn't think there is no hope," I said. "One of our Kikuyu nurses recovered from the influenza."

"They are not as delicate as Valerie," Mrs. Pritchard said. She kept looking at me. "Where did you get your red hair?" she asked. "Valerie's was from her grandfather."

"I don't know," I said. "Both my parents were orphans. They never knew their relatives."

"Never knew their relatives?" Mr. Pritchard repeated. "How very unusual."

I didn't think I could sit there for one more minute making conversation. The Pritchards with their cold, critical eyes were too much for me. Fortunately at that moment Mr. Pritchard said to his wife, "I think you should lie down, my dear. You've had no sleep in days."

I led his wife into my own bedroom. I could not bear to think of her lying on my parents' bed. She looked at the narrow camp bed with distaste. Finally, with a great sigh she settled down. "You might just wring out a cloth in cold water for my forehead," she said, but when I returned with the cloth, she was asleep. Mr. Pritchard sat alone in the sitting room with his head in his hands.

At last I was left to myself. I sat on the porch, looking out at the hospital. A starling chattered on a tree, its gaudy purple, red, and yellow feathers out of place in so much sadness. A lizard settled in the sun, and I was glad of the company. It was dusk when I saw Father walking slowly along the dirt path that led from the hospital. I ran to him, seizing hold of his hand.

He pulled away. "No, Rachel, I'm not well. I should not have come, but it is only right that I tell the Pritchards myself. We have the sorrows of Job. Their child has died. She had no chance. She was very ill."

He went into the house. I could hear loud crying that was not unlike the wailing of the Kikuyu families. The suffering was surely the same. Father and I watched as the Pritchards drove away. After a moment Father said, "If anything should happen to me, Rachel, you must contact the mission board. They will care for you. You must urge them, Rachel, to find another doctor for Tumaini. I would never rest in my grave if something should happen to the hospital." His face was pale. He looked down at me as if he would take me in his arms. "How can I leave you? It would be almost better if you were to join your mother and me." He turned and made his way slowly back to the hospital.

THREE

I repeated Father's words over and over. "It would be almost better if you were to join your mother and me." The words were terrible, worse than any threat of doom in the Old Testament. I wouldn't let myself believe in them. I stood at the window scratching at some bites on my leg from red pepper ticks and watching as the distant hills turned from lavender to purple and then darkened until I could barely make out their shape. I had not eaten since breakfast, and at last, feeling a little hungry, I roasted a sweet potato and had it with wild honey. There was nothing left then but to curl up on my bed. I shook out the covering to get rid of the last of Mrs. Pritchard. I had some idea that it was not right that I should sleep, but that I ought to keep awake and watchful. I heard the hooing and gurgle of a water-bottle bird. I listened for the lions, but they were silent on this night. The hyenas were howling. I thought of a horrible story I had heard from one of the Kikuyu. When injured, a hyena will tear at its own insides and begin to devour them. I closed my eyes tightly against the gruesome image. Afterward, because I fell asleep, I blamed myself for my father's death, as if I ought to have kept watch that night.

It was daylight and Kanoro was standing over me. In his despair he forgot his English. "*Bwana mzimu,*" he said. It was in Swahili that I learned Father had died. I am ashamed that my first thought was for myself. Like my parents before me, I was an orphan. My mind became muddled with visions of lumpy porridge and being locked into a room for misbehavior and having to wear cast-offs. I thought of David Copperfield working fourteen hours a day in a London factory. I thought of having to leave Africa. Each thought more miserable than the next. At last I came to the worst thing of all—Father was gone—and I began to sob.

It was Kanoro who comforted me and who, when the crying had at last stopped, reminded me of my responsibility. "What of the hospital?" he asked. "There are many sick there."

The nearest house with a telephone was the Pritchards' house. It was the last place I wanted to go, but I had to let the authorities in Nairobi know we had no doctor here. The mission board must be informed so that another doctor could be sent out. In the meantime, perhaps a doctor in Nairobi would come out once or twice a week to supervise the nurses and father's assistant so that the hospital could remain open.

In the oxcart it was a half-hour journey to the Pritchards'. Kanoro remained in the cart while I walked up to the Pritchards' large home. I knocked on the door, and a servant in a white jacket opened the door. When he saw me, he put his hand over his mouth to stifle a cry. After a moment he said, "I am sorry, miss. I thought our young mistress had returned to us. Please to come in."

The Pritchards' house was made of stone with a wooden roof. The servant led me to the sitting room. The draperies were drawn. In the gloom I could make out a large fireplace, a piano, overstuffed chairs and sofas, and a massive table on which stood tall silver candlesticks. Our house had hard-packed dirt floors covered with grass mats. Here the floors were of wood and covered with animal skins. As my eyes grew accustomed to the darkness, I saw that Mrs. Pritchard was seated in one of the chairs staring at me.

"I'm so sorry to bother you, but my father died in the night," I said. "I wonder if you would be kind enough to inform the officials in Nairobi. It may be that they could send a doctor to our hospital."

"Yes, of course," she said. "And what of yourself? What will you do with no parents?" I was frightened, for her look was greedy and made me think of the hyenas that follow the pregnant zebras and antelope waiting until the moment their helpless calf is born and then devour it. I could not think what she wanted of me.

"The mission board will have to be notified," I said. "I suppose they'll arrange to have me return to England."

"And then? Have you family? You said your parents were orphans."

"No. I have no family. The church has an orphanage."

"And do you wish to go there?"

I shook my head.

"Make yourself comfortable while Mr. Pritchard calls Nairobi. I'll have Njora bring you tea." She gave me one more greedy look and disappeared. A moment later the Kikuyu servant arrived with a silver tray. There was lemonade with bits of real ice floating in it and little sandwiches and chocolate biscuits all arranged neatly on a china plate as thin as eggshell. My face burned as I thought of the clumsy chipped cups in which I had served the Pritchards their tea. Though I had had nothing to eat that morning, I was too unhappy to do more than sip the lemonade and nibble at a sandwich. I was puzzled at Mrs. Pritchard's sudden kindness. It did not fit with the way she had looked at me.

I could hear the Pritchards' conversation like the murmur of whydah birds and then, more loudly, Mr. Pritchard speaking into a telephone. A few minutes later he appeared. "We are very sorry for your loss," he said.

"I've notified the hospital in Nairobi to see about a doctor keeping an eye on your hospital. They said they can do nothing. They are overworked with their own influenza cases."

I had written down the name and address of the president of the missionary board. Reluctantly I handed it to him. "Is there someone in Nairobi who could contact the board?" I tried to keep my voice steady. "To let them know what happened—and that I am here."

"Yes, yes. I'll see that a cable goes off. Just leave it to me. I have sent your servant back. Our car will take you and Mrs. Pritchard to your home. She will help you to pack, and then you must come and stay with us until some plan is made for you. I know you have a sad duty. I'll send some boys along to help with the burial of your father."

I was taken aback. I had felt very much alone, so their care was welcome, yet I had a feeling of being taken over, which frightened me. However friendless I was, I was not sure the Pritchards were the friends I needed or wanted. Their sudden concern puzzled me.

I drove back with Mrs. Pritchard. It was the first time I had been in an automobile, and for a moment the strangeness of it swept away my suspicions of the Pritchards until I overheard the Kikuyu driver and the man, Njora, who had come with him to help in the burial. They spoke in Swahili, which Mrs. Pritchard must not have learned. Perhaps they believed I did not understand it as well, or perhaps they were kind and wished to warn me without the Pritchards knowing. The driver said, "*Bwana* and *Memsahib* will devour the small one like the wild dogs swallow a little antelope."

A moment later we pulled up to my house, and there was Kanoro. He stared at me as I got out of the car with Mrs. Pritchard. Instead of hurrying to greet me as he normally would have, he stood there as if he were unsure of what to do.

Mrs. Pritchard said, "No doubt you will want your father buried next to your mother. You must tell my man where the coffin is to go. I suppose your fellow can put a coffin together? Now let's go inside and pack your things."

It was just at this moment that I should have said, "I won't pack my things. I won't go back with you. I'll stay here and wait for the mission board to tell me what to do." I didn't say it. My parents had brought me up to obey my elders. How could my parents know that one day I might be obeying the Pritchards?

I went into the house, which had never seemed so deserted. I found an old suitcase and began to pack my few belongings, conscious all the while of Mrs. Pritchard standing over me, a distasteful look on her face as she saw how worn and shabby my clothes were.

"Perhaps you had best leave all of that," she said.

I could not follow her. "What will I wear?"

I saw her face tighten. "We have suitable things at the house."

I was puzzled until I realized she was speaking of her daughter's clothes. "Oh, I couldn't," I said.

"We'll decide that later. I believe your man is at the door."

I bristled at the way she called Kanoro "your fellow" and "your man," as if he belonged to us. Kanoro must have felt her distain, for he had always come into our house as a member of the family. Now he stood uncertainly at the entrance. "We are ready," he said, not calling me by name as was usual.

When we went outside, I was startled to see hundreds of Kikuyu gathered in the churchyard. There were many familiar faces. There was the man who had recovered from a bad case of blackwater and the woman who had been cured of a snakebite and the little boy who had come to the hospital with a badly shattered arm. "Kanoro," I said, "I thought the families had all gone away because of the sickness."

"The word went out, and they have come back for your father," he said.

I threw my arms around him and wept. I felt Mrs. Pritchard pulling me away. In a harsh voice she said to Kanoro, "Tell those people to go away."

When I was the one she ordered about, I obeyed her, but I would not let her order Kanoro about. "The Kikuyu who are here are patients of my father's. They have come to honor him and must stay for his funeral."

I did not know how I had done it, but I had put into my voice something that kept Mrs. Pritchard from saying more. We walked to the churchyard, where the grave had been prepared. It was next to the grave of my mother, where my flowers were still fresh in their jar.

Kanoro handed me Father's Bible, and in a choked voice I read Father's favorite words, for he loved Tumaini: "Yea, the sparrow hath found an house, and the swallow a nest for herself." As I read the verse, I thought the sparrows and swallows were lucky with their nests, for even a bit of woven straw in a tree was better than the house of the Pritchards, where I would nest that night.

Kanoro whispered to me, "Our chief, Mabui, wishes to make a last *ngoma* for your father." A *ngoma* was a ceremonial dance, which Father had always enjoyed. My parents and I had often attended *ngoma*s. Once a visiting missionary had come and a *ngoma* was given in his honor. He was shocked. "How can you allow such a pagan celebration?" he asked. Father only smiled and said, "Surely such exultation comes from God?"

I said to Kanoro, "My father would be honored."

A circle was formed and the drums and the dancing began. The women were splendid in their beads and wire bracelets and painted faces, the men imposing with ostrich plumes, leopard-skin capes, and necklaces of lions' teeth. Just outside the circle the small children imitated their elders. Around and around the dancers went, chanting, flinging their arms about to the rhythm of the drums, the stamping sending clouds of dust into the air. Sometimes the dance was formal and stately, sometimes fiery and boisterous.

Mrs. Pritchard was horrified. "Tell them to stop at once," she hissed. "This is a disgrace."

"No," I said. "We would hurt their feelings. Father would have been very pleased. He loved their *ngomas*."

At last she could stand it no more and, reaching for my arm, began to pull me away toward the car. I only had time to break away and run to Kanoro and say my good-byes. "Please thank the Kikuyu for me," I said. A moment later the car door closed on me and I was driven away, the chanting still in my ears.

My last sight of Tumaini was of the hospital. All my life I had heard stories of how the hospital had been built with sun-dried bricks that Father had helped make. Supplies had been slow in coming from England, and Father had had to improvise or do without. The medicine men of the tribe had been jealous of him and spread rumors that kept away patients who desperately needed Father's help. His first clinic had been held under the trees. Mother had had to deal with rats and cockroaches and scorpions that climbed into our shoes at night. Until the well had been dug, water had come from the river or from the rainwater barrel, and every ounce had to be boiled. Father and Mother had never given up.

When we reached the Pritchards' house, Mr. Pritchard asked his wife, "Did you manage the funeral all right? I suppose it was a sad affair." He had a glass in his hand and his words were slurred.

"It was not quite what I would have chosen," Mrs. Pritchard said. I could see that she was anxious to tell her husband of the scandalous *ngoma*, for she hurried me and my things into a bedroom. "You will have Valerie's room," she said. "You must be tired after your ordeal. Perhaps you should rest for a bit." With that she left me.

My first thought was of the girl whose room it had been. I felt that Valerie was looking down at me, angry at my trespassing. Though I wanted to, I was afraid to stretch out on the bed, for it was spread with a silk counterpane. Instead I settled into a chair and looked about me. It was a girl's room such as you might read of in a book about a princess. It was all silk and ruffles, with pretty pictures of scenes of what I guessed must be the English countryside. The only thing in all the room that was the least out of place was a picture on Valerie's dresser of an elderly man. He had white hair and an old-fashioned mutton-chop beard. He was frowning as if he were furious at having his picture taken. I wondered at so stern a picture in this pretty and graceful room.

I could hardly understand all that had happened to me,

one terrible thing after the other. First Mother and then Father. Now I was with strangers I disliked and did not trust. My future as an orphan could only mean I must make a long, lonely journey back to a land I had never seen and be shut up in some institution where I would be one child among many. I would be dependent upon charity for every bite I ate.

After a bit Njora, with a pitying look on his face, brought me a jug of hot water, and I washed my face and hands in a flowered bowl and put on a dress that in these grand surroundings appeared more worn and shabby than ever. I had forgotten my comb and brush, and a glance in the mirror showed me how untidy my hair was. Without thinking I reached for the comb on the dresser and began to run it through my hair. It was like a live snake in my hands and I dropped it at once. It was not my comb; it was Valerie's.

Mrs. Pritchard came into the room without knocking. She was wearing a green dress of some sheer material. There was a frill of lace at her throat and on her sleeves. I thought it odd she was not in some dark color, some color more suitable for mourning. She looked at my worn dress and gave a little shrug, as if I were beyond help. "Dinner is ready, my dear. Perhaps you would like to put on one of Valerie's frocks. We dress for dinner here."

I shook my head.

When she hesitated, I was afraid she would force one of

the dead girl's dresses over my head. "Well, perhaps we'll let it go for this first night," she said.

As we entered the dining room, Mr. Pritchard stood, a little unsteadily, napkin in hand, until we were seated. He had a glass in front of him, which he drained and refilled from a glass bottle at his place. There was no such glass bottle at Mrs. Pritchard's place or at my place.

Njora carried in a large covered bowl of soup, which Mrs. Pritchard ladled into bowls. The bowls had a gold edging. I looked to see what spoon, from among the many, Mrs. Pritchard picked up and I did the same. Though the soup was tasty, I could not force more than a spoonful or two down my throat.

Mr. Pritchard said, "I have cabled the mission board that your parents have succumbed to the influenza epidemic."

I took a deep breath. "And you told them of me?"

Mr. Pritchard's glance slid away. "Oh, yes," he said. "And I have received an answering cable. I am afraid it is not encouraging. Because of the recent war, there's a shortage of missionary doctors at the moment. Many went to the front and many did not return. They have no one to send. It appears the hospital must close."

Father and Mother's hard work would be for nothing. I thought of Kanoro and Ita and Wanja and Jata and all the men and women whom Father and Mother had trained. Where would they go? Perhaps to the native hospital in

Nairobi, but their families would not be able to accompany them. Only Africans who had jobs in the city were allowed to live there. I didn't think they would be happy in the city of Nairobi without their families. I did not know how, but I promised myself that there would be a hospital again at Tumaini. Then I realized there had been no mention of me. "When will I be sent for?" I asked.

"We need not worry about that for the moment. You are quite safe here."

With my worry over the hospital and the strangeness all around me, I didn't realize that Mr. Pritchard had not answered my question.

There was the sound of a motorcar on the road. Mr. and Mrs. Pritchard looked at each other. Quickly Mrs. Pritchard got up from the table. "Rachel, come along to your room. This has been a sad day for you—you must get some rest." Though her words were full of concern for me, I saw that she was flustered and anxious to get me out of the way. The moment I was safely in the room, she closed the door and hurriedly left me.

Unseen hands had turned down the bed and laid out a nightdress of fine muslin trimmed in lace with narrow blue ribbons drawn though the neck and sleeves. It was a nightdress I might have dreamed of if I had had a notion such things existed, but I could not put on the gown of the poor, dead Valerie.

Car doors opened and slammed shut. Wondering if

some official were coming to inquire about the hospital, I went to the window and looked out. The window of my room was near the entrance. I saw a couple I did not recognize. The woman wore an elegant long linen coat and a large straw hat trimmed with flowers that jounced about as she walked up to the entrance. The man had on a white linen suit and wore a panama hat. The Pritchards were at the door to greet them. The woman said, "We're so relieved to find you up and about. I can't tell you how many in Nairobi are ill. I don't see Valerie. I hope she's all right."

"Oh, yes, Valerie is fine," Mrs. Pritchard said. "I put her to bed early tonight. I don't want her overtired and susceptible to this terrible illness. She leaves at the end of the week, you know, to go to her grandfather's in England. I can't think how we'll manage without her."

"Have you heard about the missionary hospital?" Mr. Pritchard asked of the couple. "Wiped out, I'm afraid. I was there today to see they had a decent burial. The parents and the child, all dead."

Mrs. Pritchard said, "No need to stand here chattering. Come in and Aldon will make you one of his famous pink gins. It's a great nuisance, but we've had to send all but our cook and one of our servants away until the scare is over. We don't want to take the chance of bringing the disease into the house." The voices faded.

"All dead," Mr. Pritchard had said. "The parents and the child, all dead."

I sank down onto the bed. What could it mean? Mrs. Pritchard had said quite clearly that Valerie was alive. I almost believed her, for here I was in Valerie's room, sitting on her bed. Had the Pritchards given me some magic potion that had turned me into Valerie like Alice in Wonderland? In stories Mother had read to me of the missionaries in India there were tales of reincarnation, where dead people came back as someone else. I pinched myself. I was very real. I looked into the mirror over the washstand. It was my face, not Valerie's.

FOUR

I was so afraid I would turn into the poor dead girl, I would not put on her nightdress. Njora, when he came in the morning with my hot water for washing, was startled, for I had slept all night on the floor rather than get into Valerie's bed. I had not slept so much as I had tossed and turned and worried about what would happen to me.

"Njora," I asked in Swahili, "Valerie has really died, hasn't she? It is not a dream."

"No, *Msabu*. I am to tell no one, but I tell you because you already know."

He would say no more but only told me that breakfast was waiting for me.

With all my sorrows and worries I had not thought to eat a bite of breakfast, but when I saw the dishes filled with eggs and bacon and ham and little pots of jams and jellies

49

and thick pats of butter, I could not help myself. The Pritchards seemed pleased at my appetite.

In a hearty voice Mr. Pritchard said, "Well, well, nothing like a good night's sleep. Now if you will excuse me, I have some things to attend to."

Mrs. Pritchard urged more food on me, but as he left the room I saw Mr. Pritchard and his wife exchange a knowing look, a look that took away my appetite. I remembered the puzzling things they had said to the visitors the night before. Suddenly it seemed important for me to escape. Gathering all my strength, I said, "I think I had better return home until someone comes for me and tells me where I must go."

Mrs. Pritchard pulled her chair closer to me and began to speak in what she must have thought was a kindly tone, but which sounded false in my ears. "Rachel, my dear, you have it in your power to do a great kindness to an elderly gentleman. More than a great kindness. It would not be an exaggeration to say you could save the dear man's life."

Her words made no sense to me. I had helped out in the hospital, but I surely wouldn't know how to save a life.

Mrs. Pritchard leaned closer to me. I could smell the heavy fragrance of her perfume, so strong it almost smothered me. "I believe I told you that Valerie was to visit her grandfather in England." At the mention of her daughter's name, Mrs. Pritchard's eyes became bleary with tears and she had to stop for a moment. After a bit she went on. "Our daughter was to leave here for England at the end of the week. Her grandfather has been very ill. It is only the expectation of Valerie's visit that has kept the dear man alive. Valerie is everything to him, and news of her death would be the end of him. We want you to go in her place."

"He would not be pleased to see me. It's your daughter he wants."

"You *would* be our daughter. You would be Valerie."

"I don't look like her. He would know I wasn't Valerie."

Mrs. Pritchard's eyes narrowed. "My husband's father has never seen Valerie, only pictures of her. We could say that you had been ill and had lost weight. You have the family's red hair. Of course Valerie was a very graceful and accomplished child." This time tears rolled down Mrs. Pritchard's cheeks, and I could see they were real tears and once again I felt sorry for her.

"I don't suppose you can play the piano?"

"Oh, yes. I can play hymns."

"Oh, well, perhaps there would be no need for piano playing." She sighed. "It would not be difficult for you. Grandfather lives in a large mansion in the middle of a park with great trees that are centuries old. We used to live there before we were sent—that is, before we came to Africa. Surely, my dear, that would be a better place for you, with someone who loves you and would give you everything you wished. Much better than some cold and miserable orphanage where you would be trained for a job that would bring you a lifetime of unhappiness."

Mrs. Pritchard was watching me. "I have such a sad picture in my head," she said, "of dear Grandfather ill and alone in that great house receiving a notice of Valerie's death. I see him clasping the letter to his heart and, with a great sigh, taking his last breath."

Mrs. Pritchard studied my reaction to the unhappy story, which I thought, like everything about her, exaggerated and probably untrue. Yet suppose it was a little true. If it was something that was possible for me to do, why should I not do it? Why should I not make the grandfather happy? Certainly living in a great mansion if only for a few days was better than a cold, mean orphanage.

My conscience began to be busy. "It would be a lie," the conscience said, "and you know it. What would your parents say?" It is not hard to silence a conscience. Though I did not entirely believe Mrs. Pritchard's words, still I could not put out of my mind the sad picture of the lonely old man clutching the letter that told him of his granddaughter's death. I saw myself walking through the door of the room in which he was sitting and his face lighting up. He would put his arms around me. All the servants would be standing by saying they had never seen their master look so well and how it was a miracle. And at least for a short time I would not have to go to the orphanage.

"I don't know," I said. "I think it would be wrong."

"Nonsense," Mrs. Pritchard said. "It is your Christian duty. If you could save the poor man and you chose not to, it would be as bad as murder."

Murder! To be accused of murdering someone was certainly worse than a lie. "How long would I stay there?"

"Only as long as Grandfather lives. A short time."

In a last desperate effort I stammered, "But, Mrs. Pritchard, I don't think I should go. I'm not Valerie."

"That has nothing to do with it." She stood up. "Well, let us consider that it is all settled. You'll be leaving in three days. Your railway and steamer tickets were purchased long ago by Mr. Pritchard's father, but we have a great deal of work ahead of us. Your grandfather will have questions, and you must have answers. Now, while you finish your breakfast, I'll begin the packing. Unfortunately just when we need them, our servants have been sent away."

It wasn't settled in my head at all. It would be the end of me, the end of Rachel. I would disappear as surely as if I had been snapped up by a wild dog's jaws. Yet what would that Rachel be who lived in an orphanage, was allowed no special friend, ate lumpy porridge, and spent the rest of her life scrubbing floors? Surely that would not be me either.

So much had happened. Mother and Father gone. The hospital to close. I myself carried away from my home. For the moment I did not see how I could fight the Pritchards, but desperately I hung on to Rachel Sheridan.

My lessons began at once and went on morning, afternoon, and night for three miserable days. Mrs. Pritchard
had begun, "Your name is Valerie Agnes Pritchard. Mr.
Pritchard's father had two sons. The elder son died in the
war and left no family. Mr. Pritchard is his second son. If Mr.
Pritchard's father were a just man, Mr. Pritchard would be
in England preparing to take over the estate. Unfortunately
Mr. Pritchard's father is prejudiced against him."

"Prejudiced?"

"Mr. Pritchard had some difficulties as a young man,
and his father has never forgiven him. It is very unjust. Mr.
Pritchard should be in possession of the estate at this
moment instead of having to rely on his father for every
penny, selfish old man that he is."

When Mrs. Pritchard saw the shocked look on my face,
she added, "Of course he will be generous to you—he has
been already. And the day that he dies, a day that cannot
be too far away, I am sure we will be remembered." She
looked off into the distance, as if she could see that pleasant day when the grandfather should be dead.

She turned back to me. "We have heard rumors about his
money and the estate going to some organization for birds,
but no one in his right mind would do such a thing. If you
endear yourself to the old man, things may come right."

We went through the family album. "You must learn
who everyone is. Of course Valerie was born in Africa, as
you were, so she never actually met any of her relations,

but Valerie knew who they were. They are all gone now, so there is no possibility of your seeing them. Valerie hated Africa and like Mr. Pritchard and me couldn't wait to go to England. There is no elegance here in Africa, no decent society. It was no place to raise a sensitive child."

Talking of Valerie had made Mrs. Pritchard very unhappy. Tears slid down her cheeks. I reached to take her hand, but she drew it away.

"I'm quite all right," she said. "We must get on with our lesson."

My head was being stuffed with bits of information about the Pritchard family and life on the Pritchard plantation. But I could not forget something Mrs. Pritchard had said earlier. I asked, "If you and Mr. Pritchard are so anxious to return to England, why weren't you going back with Valerie?"

Mrs. Pritchard stared at me for a moment. "That is not possible," she said, and quickly went on to make me memorize Valerie's birth date and the birthdays of Mr. Pritchard and herself. "It may be that you can remind your grandfather to remember us on those dates. He has a great deal of money and could be more forthcoming than he is."

I had believed that once I left for England, I need not have anything else to do with the Pritchards, but now I saw my mistake. The Pritchards were two great spiders in the middle of a web, and the threads of the web would reach all the way to England and hold me fast. They would send letters to their daughter, and it would appear odd if I did not answer the letters. I would be expected to coax presents from the grandfather. I, who loved Africa, was to be Valerie who hated Africa. I couldn't do it. I said nothing, but on the third day I resolved on another plan.

That afternoon I complained of being tired and asked if I might lie down for a bit.

"Good heavens!" Mrs. Pritchard said, a frightened look on her face. She drew away from me. "You're not coming down with influenza?"

"No. I'm only a little confused by all there is to learn."

"Yes, I understand. You've had terrible losses, and now this. It's all happening too quickly. After this is over, you and I will both have time to do our grieving. Lie down until dinner."

For a moment I almost felt kindly toward Mrs. Pritchard, but then she said, "You will need to be strong, for Grandfather is a forceful man."

It sounded as if she were sending me to war. I was determined to run away. The moment I was in my room, I changed into my khaki pants and bush shirt and climbed out the window. Looking first to be sure I wasn't seen, I hurried along the road that would take me to Tumaini. I knew the dangers. I had been warned a hundred times about being alone in the bush, but I believed the Pritchards were more deadly, more dangerous than anything that might leap out at me.

First I had to travel through a swampy patch where papyrus and reeds crept up to the road. A weaverbird was busy with its nest in a banana tree. A lizard was sunning itself. I knew it was a place for snakes, and I hurried along. Overhead I heard the *keewee, keewee* of an eagle, but when I looked up it was only a dot in the sky. When I saw a black-headed heron stalking frogs, its sharp beak impaling them, I thought at once of Mrs. Pritchard as the heron and myself as the frog. The road as it climbed out of the swamp and onto the plain was so narrow that I brushed against the thornbushes, getting prickers in my legs. The desert rose was blooming. I had been warned against picking the blooms, for the sap was poison. When they go out to hunt, the Kikuyu dip their arrows into the sap. I thought the desert rose was like the life the Pritchards were offering me. There would be the handsome house and the riches, and at their center the poison of the Pritchards' greed.

The grasses alongside the road were taller than I was, so there was no knowing what might be hidden there. I saw the snaky neck and bald head of an ostrich move along and then disappear. A duiker, a male, sporting a short horn, was nibbling at the grass. The wind was against me and the duiker had not yet picked up my scent. There was a movement in the tall grasses ahead of me. I froze. I saw the grasses bend and then spring up again as some invisible creature slithered along close to the ground. A flash of gold shot out of the grass and sprang at the duiker. The duiker collapsed onto the ground, the leopard clinging to its back. A moment later the leopard was tearing at the little antelope's flesh.

I ran until my throat burned and I had no more breath. If the duiker, a fatter meal than I would have been, had not been there, the leopard would have made do with me. I had never been so alone. I felt like the only person on the whole continent of Africa. Sweat poured onto my face so that I had to blink my eyes to see. My heels were blistered, and every step hurt. Flies nibbled at the back of my neck. The thorns in my legs stung, but I didn't dare stop to remove them.

When I came at last to Tumaini, I saw our home was deserted and only a few families were camped about the hospital. In the three days I had been gone, the grass had sprung up, nearly hiding the path from our house to the hospital. The rains, the hot sun, and the insects would soon claim Tumaini. I slipped into the house without being seen and came face to face with Kanoro, who cried out as if he had seen a ghost. Slowly he reached out a hand and touched me.

I threw my arms around him and we clung to each other. He held me, patting my head as he had done when I was a child. "Oh, can it be you, Rachel? We all believed you were dead. We saw them bury you."

"What do you mean?"

"Yesterday Mr. Pritchard and his man came with a coffin and buried it in the churchyard beside the grave of your parents. When we saw that, all our hope left us. There will be a great rejoicing when it is known that you are well and alive."

I dried my eyes and looked around. "Kanoro, where is everyone?"

"There are only a few people remaining in the hospital. An official from the government in Nairobi came and said the hospital would be closed and everyone must leave."

"Where will everyone go?" I asked.

"We go back to our *shambas*. I only stay here to watch over your parents' things."

"Kanoro, I don't trust the Pritchards."

"No one trusts them. They sent away all their servants, only keeping in their home two men who would do their bidding. It was those men who came here with the coffin saying it was you."

"Kanoro, show me the grave."

"Who would want to look upon her own grave?"

"Show me, Kanoro."

There next to my parents' grave was a cross with my name: Rachel Sheridan 1906–1919.

"Kanoro," I said, "I want to go away with you and your people."

"Oh, child, that can't be." The wrinkles appeared on his forehead. "The government men in Nairobi would say we

took you away. They would come after us and shut us up
in their jail. We would be like animals in a cage."

Kanoro was right. My plan had been a foolish one with
no thought for anyone but myself. There was something
else as well. I saw that I had become unlucky. Everyone
around me had died. I was thought to have died myself.
Like my red hair, I would be seen as dangerous. Much as I
wanted to escape the Pritchards, I knew it was impossible.
I would go to England, and if the truth were discovered
there, even a jail in England would be better than another
day with the Pritchards.

"There is no one coming from the mission board,
Kanoro. Divide everything among the hospital staff. The
pots and pans will be useful, and Father's tools. But
Kanoro, I promise I'll come back one day and the hospital
will be just as it was. One thing. You must not tell anyone
that you saw me. They must think me dead. Now I have to
go back to the Pritchards."

Kanoro said, "You should not have made the trip alone
through the bush. I will go back with you." When he had
pulled the thorns from my legs and bandaged my blistered heels, he took up Father's rifle, holding it proudly,
and together we retraced my steps with no adventure
except for a porcupine that sent up its quills at the sight
of us and then waddled away. When the Pritchard house
came into view, Kanoro stopped abruptly, as if the house
might cast an evil spell on him.

"Rachel, you are like my own child. How can I let you go into that place? The people in there are like buzzards. They will peck at you until nothing is left."

I tried to comfort him. "Tomorrow I leave for England and I'll never have to see the Pritchards again." I threw my arms around him.

Kanoro held me for a long moment and then said to me, "However far you go from here, you must carry me with you in your heart. If you are lonely, you must know that every hour I will be thinking of you. If you are among evil people, you must be like the lion, gathering your strength and awaiting your time. That time will come, and when it comes, you will come back to us."

Though I had little hope, I promised. "I will come back, Kanoro."

A moment later I was inside the Pritchards' house, where a furious Mrs. Pritchard took me by both arms and began to shake me until my teeth chattered.

"You foolish girl. Where did you sneak off to? We have looked everywhere for you. Has anyone seen you? What were you thinking? You could have ruined everything for us. We rescue you from a miserable orphanage and give you a chance to be someone, and this is the thanks we get."

Mr. Pritchard freed me. "The girl is back, Emma, and she leaves tomorrow. There is nothing to be gained by such talk." The threatening look he gave me was worse than any shaking. In a menacing voice he said, "I am sure,

Rachel, that it will not happen again. Now go to your room and tidy yourself for dinner."

It could not happen again. When I walked into my bedroom, I saw that the window now had bars across it.

BOOK TWO

Valerie Pritchard

FIVE

$\mathcal{M}$rs. Pritchard was to accompany me on the train that would take me on the overnight trip from Nairobi to Mombasa, where I would board the ship. For three days I had resisted wearing Valerie's clothes, but now I had to put them on. Mrs. Pritchard herself had altered the clothes to fit me, sitting by the hour, tears dropping onto the silks and linens as she took in seams and shortened hems. Seeing her unhappiness, my dislike began to melt away. I said, "I know how you feel about your daughter. I think of my mother and father all the time."

She gave me a bitter look. "Older people must expect to die; Valerie was only a child."

There was no comforting her.

I sat in the train, miserable in the dead girl's clothes with a cold and silent Mrs. Pritchard beside me. Though she had urged me for days to wear her daughter's clothes, when at last she saw them on me, there was so furious a look of resentment on her face, I was afraid that, as in the story of the shirt woven as a curse by an evil woman, Valerie's clothes would wrap around me and burn me.

As we left Nairobi, we traveled along the Athi River with its thick grasses and herds of animals. After a restless night I awoke to the desolate Taru, an area of grassless land. Africa was hurrying by as if someone were turning the pages of a book too quickly. I was miserable at what I was leaving behind. Even the railway itself had a sad story. When it was being built, many of the men brought from India to work on it were devoured by lions. I felt my own future would be no better.

Mombasa was an island with harbors and ships everywhere you looked. On its eastern shore was the Indian Ocean, which appeared to me to have no ending. We spent the night in a small hotel near the railway station. I shared a room with Mrs. Pritchard. She said it was for economy's sake, but I believe she did not want to let me out of her sight. The great lump beside me in a white nightdress was so frightening, I didn't close my eyes all night. At breakfast Mrs. Pritchard sent back her poached eggs because they were too runny. When new ones appeared, there was a great fuss because the eggs were too hard. As she scolded the poor waiter, I scrunched down in my chair and wished I were invisible.

We took a taxi across the city to the ship, which looked

to me as large as Noah's ark, but Mrs. Pritchard was scornful. "It's little more than a tramp steamer," she said, "made to carry sisal and coffee, not passengers. The passenger steamers carried troops during the war and are being refitted."

I was introduced to Miss Limplinger, a governess whose charges had outgrown her, and who was returning to England. Mrs. Pritchard had made arrangements for Miss Limplinger to share my stateroom on the voyage and to watch over me. The woman was tall and so thin that even through her clothes you could make out the sharp angles of elbows and knees. Her eyes were very bright and inquisitive, like a bird hunting among the grasses for insects.

She seemed delighted to have me in her care, as if she missed having children to order about. "Just leave her to me, Mrs. Pritchard," she said. "I know all about young girls. I can promise you she will be in very good hands." As if to prove her point, she took a firm grip on my arm.

"I am sure she'll give you no trouble," Mrs. Pritchard said. She leaned down and gave me a cold kiss. "Good-bye, my dear. Your grandfather's solicitor will cable us when you arrive. Write at once and let us know how your dear grandfather is." She gave me a long look that made me think of the leopard pouncing upon the little duiker. When the ship pulled out and she became no more than a speck on the shore, I breathed a great sigh of relief.

The harbor was crowded with every kind of boat. There were hundreds of dhows, their sails billowing out in the breeze. Mombasa was a city of traders, and the little boats would sail with their cargos up and down the African coast and even to India. In the distance I could make out Mombasa's ancient coral fort looming over the harbor. In my history lessons I had learned that the fort, built by the Portuguese in the sixteenth century, was the scene of one bloody battle after another. First, all the Portuguese there were killed. When more Portuguese came and took back the fort, all the new Portuguese were killed by the sultan of Zanzibar, and then the Africans got rid of the Arabs and then the Arabs came back until the British took over the fort. Now it was a prison. I felt I was a prisoner myself and wished the fort with its bloody history had not been my last sight of Africa.

A flurry of gulls swooped and shrieked above us. "Those are the same gulls you will see this summer in England," Miss Limplinger said.

"And then in the fall the gulls will return to Africa?" I asked.

"Yes, indeed," she said.

I thought the gulls very lucky, for by then the grandfather would have died and I would be in an English orphanage.

On board ship everything was unfamiliar, including myself. I was called Valerie now and asked questions about my childhood in Africa. I had to choke back any mention of my father and mother, of Kanoro, of the hospital and the Kikuyu, all the things that were dear to me. Some of the passengers had met or heard of the Pritchards, and I had to watch every word I said. Sometimes I had no answer to a question, and then I learned to look very sad and the person who asked the question would apologize: "Of course; you are homesick and I shouldn't have brought all that up."

I had thought I would have the long voyage to find myself again and to decide how I could tell the grandfather the truth without killing him. Instead I had Miss Limplinger buzzing like a mosquito in my ear. I longed to stand looking out across the wide, empty sea with its hidden creatures just below the surface like wild animals concealed in tall grass, but Miss Limplinger followed me everywhere. She had been told to keep an eye on me, and she would do her duty.

When we took our meals, Miss Limplinger was careful to look about the table to see if there was someone important or aristocratic. Finding such a person, she would grovel and bow and scrape. She would stick to them after dinner when we went into the salon for coffee. I saw that many of the passengers liked being fawned over. She was like the egrets that perch on the backs of the hippos, living on the hippos' lice and pleasing the hippos who found their attentions useful.

Miss Limplinger was anxious to let me know that she was not looked upon as a servant, but considered one of the family. "The Govetts, who employed me, took me everywhere," she said. To prove her point she was full of gossip about the people she had met. This one was not as well-off as he seemed, that one was distantly related to the husband of the king's wife's sister, another one was dying of some terrible disease. There was much chatter about what all the women wore: "Her skirt well above her ankles!"

I paid no attention to these stories until one afternoon she said, "I once saw your parents in Nairobi at a Government House garden party. I can't be sure, but I do believe you were with them. One doesn't forget ginger hair, although I don't recall you as being so thin. Of course I never for a moment believed the tales of your father being disowned and sent away by your grandfather. That was just malicious talk, I am sure."

I didn't believe it was malicious talk. Hadn't Mrs. Pritchard almost said as much before she had caught herself? What did that mean? Was the grandfather truly looking forward to my visiting, or was I being forced on him, the first step in the Pritchards' desire to return to England? Would my coming truly make him better, or would this reminder of a son he had had to send away cause him more misery?

After our lunches I would have my one moment of solitude and peace to consider all this. Miss Limplinger settled onto a deck chair with a book and assigned me the seat next to her, giving me a book to read as well, but after a bit she drifted off to sleep and I was free for an hour to think my own thoughts. On this day, after hearing that Mr. Pritchard might have been sent to Africa as a result of some mischief, I determined to work out a plan for my arrival. I knew Miss Limplinger was to turn me over to the grandfather's solicitor. The moment I was alone with him, I would tell my story. I didn't care if he sent me to an orphanage—all that mattered to me was finding my way back to the truth. Living day after day with a lie was like carrying around a great burden that I longed to set down.

The resolve that I would soon speak the truth was the fragile raft that kept me afloat all those long days upon the sea. And the days were long. All my life I had been free to wander about; now I was imprisoned in a room no larger than a closet with Miss Limplinger hovering over me like a hawk over a pigeon.

She chose my clothes and my food. She showed me fond letters she had received from children who had once been in her charge. I saw that she could not understand why I kept my distance from her, why I did not open my heart to her, but there was a terrible lie between us and I could not reach across it. I thought of confiding in her, but her love of gossip held me back. I was afraid my sad tale would be nothing more than a story she would whisper to her next charge.

Each day I was a little farther from the Africa I loved. Occasionally the ship would dock to take on or put off cargo. We stopped in Alexandria, Egypt. I had read about Egypt's pyramids and Cleopatra and the great ancient library in Alexandria that was burned along with all its irreplaceable books. I longed to see Egypt, if for no other reason than to place my feet on its soil, but Miss Limplinger said the country was unhealthy and full of thieves and we kept to our stateroom. We stopped in Naples, but it was in the middle of the night and I had only a glimpse from our stateroom porthole of Mount Vesuvius at dawn. There was snow on the top of the mountain, and I thought of Mount Kenya and how far away it was.

It was the end of February, and as we approached England, the air became colder and colder and I realized I had no warm coat. When we sat in our deck chairs, we wrapped ourselves in blankets. When Miss Limplinger spoke, the cold air turned her words into little clouds of smoke as if she were a dragon. The day we landed in Southampton, I saw my first snow. It was as if the snow had finally come down from Mount Kenya and was swirling all around us. I could not think what I was doing in so frigid a country. I was as cold inside as out, for my secret lay in my heart like a chip of ice.

"We are passing Portsmouth," Miss Limplinger said. "And that is Southsea Castle." She pointed out a great pile of stone in the distance. There was real excitement in her voice, and I think she was truly happy to return to England.

"Is the war not over?" I asked, for there were battleships everywhere.

"Portsmouth is a naval base," Miss Limplinger answered. "The town is always crowded with sailors, and a loutish lot they are; however, we will be docking in Southampton."

Our ship sailed along a great breakwater that must have been a mile long. There were old towers and forts along the shore and, as we reached Southampton, wharf after wharf crowded with every kind of ship and barge.

"The armies of King Henry V boarded their ships here to invade France," Miss Limplinger said. There was a note of regret in her voice, and I felt sure she was sorry no great fleet was in the harbor about to set off against France.

The grandfather's solicitor, Mr. Grumbloch, was at the dock to meet us. He was dressed all in black, and sitting on his head was a round black hat shaped like an overturned bowl. He peered out at me from thick round glasses, but the odd hat, the black clothes, and the thickness of the glasses could not disguise the bluest eyes I had ever seen. He was like the red and yellow barbet that nests among the low bushes to hide its bright colors.

His first words were "Is that thin coat all you have? Well, I'm not surprised. It is just like your father to leave it to us to clothe you properly." He thanked Miss Limplinger and handed her an envelope. From the eager way she took it, I was sure there was money inside, and I understood that she had been paid to care for me and had not done it from any kindness. I had been no more than a package to be handed over for a price. Still I was reluctant to say good-bye to her, for she was my last tie with Africa, but as soon as the envelope was tucked into her purse, she was gone with only a quick farewell.

Mr. Grumbloch took me by the arm. "I had not thought my duties would include clothing a child, but I should be deficient in my responsibilities if I were to let you freeze to death. Come along."

I was hustled into a large black automobile that reminded me of the big black beetles that scuttled about among the grasses. "Your grandfather has sent Nivers with his car to collect you and take us to Stagsway." A man in a uniform, whom I took to be Nivers, tried not to stare at me, but his curiosity got the better of him. He was a small man and precise in his way of opening car doors and tucking a blanket around me. There was a streak of gray in his black hair, so he looked a little like a badger. He said, "Welcome to England, Miss Valerie."

I had just set foot on England and already two people were deceived. I meant to get to the truth at once. As soon as he found out I was an imposter, there would be no more polite greetings of welcome or buying of coats.

When Mr. Grumbloch had settled beside me and had

straightened his hat, which had been knocked to one side in his getting in the car, I said, "I have something I must tell you."

"I have no time and no wish to hear what it is your parents are asking for now; all that must wait. You must see your grandfather at once or you will not see him alive. He is holding on to his last breath so that he can set eyes on you before he dies. He hopes to find you are not as bad as he fears, and I trust you will not disappoint him." The blue eyes fastened upon me.

I choked back the truth. It would have to wait. If I told the grandfather upon his deathbed that his son had deceived him and that I was an imposter, I would certainly hasten his death. I would truly be a murderer, just as Mrs. Pritchard had threatened. I would wait, and after his death I would return the coat.

We drove through a huge arched gateway and turned onto Southampton's High Street. The street was lined with small gabled houses and shops such as I had seen in pictures of England. Mr. Grumbloch rapped on the window that separated the backseat from Nivers, and Nivers pulled over. "Come along, now, my dear," Mr. Grumbloch said. "We'll get you suited up."

I trailed along behind him and into a shop whose windows displayed women's clothes. A shopgirl hurried up to us, and Mr. Grumbloch ordered, "Something in a warm coat for this young lady. It needn't be fancy."

But it was fancy, a soft dark-blue wool with a blue velvet collar and cuffs and a sweeping skirt down to my ankles. As the shopgirl slipped it on me, the chill I had felt since I had set foot in England disappeared, but I shook my head. I knew it must be expensive, and why should money be spent on me when in a few days I would be sent away?

In an impatient voice Mr. Grumbloch said, "What's the matter? I suppose you want something more fashionable, a bit of fur or something."

"No. Something simpler, less costly, please."

The shopgirl and Mr. Grumbloch stared at me. "Nonsense," Mr. Grumbloch said. "We'll take the coat and the young lady will wear it."

In the car he studied me and at last said, "Let me be plain with you, Valerie. I was against your coming. I knew your parents were waiting their turn. I warned your grandfather that once the camel's head was inside the tent, there would be no keeping the rest of him out. I went along with it only so that your grandfather should die in peace, but I won't be fooled by your pretending to some sort of humble and modest behavior. Your letters to your grandfather have been a disgrace, nothing but whining and begging for money. There is no chance that your parents will be allowed to come here. Your father disgraced the family with his shameful drinking and gambling. Your grandfather makes him a generous allowance, and that is all he will receive. As to the estate, you need have no hopes there. After your grandfather's death everything goes to the Royal Bird Society. There will be no talking your grandfather out of that, so you needn't try."

I cringed at his words, shrinking against the far side of the seat as if I had been attacked by warrior ants. I longed to fling open the car door and jump out, but we were traveling through empty, snowy fields. I had no money and no place to go. And if I should run away, there would be no peaceful death for the grandfather, only more misery and worry. I couldn't keep tears from sliding down my cheeks. I thought of how Father had said it would almost be better if I were to die along with him and Mother and wished for a moment it had been so.

"There, now," Mr. Grumbloch said. "I didn't mean to be harsh. Doubtless it's not your fault that your parents are greedy and underhanded. Some of that was bound to rub off on you. I only ask that you make no demands of your grandfather in his weakness but leave him to die in peace."

I longed to tell Mr. Grumbloch that my true parents were the very opposite of the Pritchards and that I meant to take nothing from the grandfather. Instead, I sat silent while mile after mile of unfamiliar country rolled past, each mile taking me closer and closer to the moment when I would have to deceive Valerie's dying grandfather. If Mr. Grumbloch was severe with me now, what would he say when he learned the truth? In spite of the coat, the cold crept from the snow-covered fields and settled into my bones. Once Mother had read a story to me in which a child was shivering with the cold. "What is shivering?" I had asked Mother. "Like the chills of malaria," she said. Still I had not been able to understand. Now at last I understood.

SIX

We turned down a winding lane that ran between two rows of tall trees. A flock of large black birds shot up into the sky. A rabbit watched us pass. "Is this some sort of park?" I asked.

"No, no," Mr. Grumbloch said. "It's all part of the Pritchard estate." The roadway curved this way and that, so I didn't see the house until we were upon it. "That is Stagsway," Mr. Grumbloch said.

At first I couldn't believe it was someone's home. I thought it must be a great church, like one of the English cathedrals I had seen in pictures. It was all gables and chimneys, and so large it seemed impossible that it should be a home for just one person. The front of the house was made of a kind of white plaster. Crisscrossing the plaster were timbers set to make a design. Beyond the house were acres of trees, and beyond the trees rolling fields. It appeared tame and peaceful, not at all like the African bush. I could not imagine a leopard lying in wait among those snow-covered fields.

An elderly man in a black suit stood at the entrance. I was so used to the white suits of the planters and the bright colors of the African men's blankets that it looked to me as if all English men were in mourning. The elderly man shuffled down a wide stairway to meet us. As he opened the car door for us, I could hear him trying to catch his breath. Mr. Grumbloch asked, "How is Mr. Pritchard, Burker?"

"I'm afraid he is very weak, sir, but looking forward to seeing the young mistress. We are very pleased to have you, Miss Valerie." Here was the third person to be deceived.

As we climbed the stairway to the entrance, he hurried along beside us, puffing and panting like a faithful old dog. My own breath disappeared as we entered the house, for we stepped into a hall many times the size of our entire house in Africa. The ceiling soared several stories. The walls were paneled in a dark wood, and halfway up one of the walls was a narrow balcony. The floors were covered with faded carpets. A fireplace big as a hippopotamus was on one side of the room and a long table stretched along the other wall. Here and there were high-backed chairs large enough for giants. Out of the corner of my eye, I could see peeking around a screen the heads of some women wearing aprons and fancy caps. At an indignant look from Burker, they quickly disappeared.

"See to these, Arthur." Burker handed our coats to a young man in a sort of uniform who blushed as he took them.

Mr. Grumbloch led me up a stairway, and as Burker trailed behind us, I could hear his knees creaking. A large lion was carved onto each of two massive stairway posts. I thought of how Kanoro had told me that I must be like the lion, gathering my strength and awaiting my time.

The steps were steep, and as I climbed I held on to the banister, feeling like Jacob climbing the ladder that reached to heaven. We came to a landing and a long hallway. Burker swept open a door, and I looked into a darkened bedroom. Lying upon an enormous bed hung with velvet draperies was the man in the picture in Valerie's room. The outline of his shape in the bed was long and thin. His expression was very severe. I thought him so like a Masai warrior, I felt the Masai greeting, *sobai*, coming to my lips. When I looked more closely, I saw that beneath the severity was a look of hopelessness and defeat. It was the look of a Masai who has been shut into a prison.

"Here she is, Hobart," Mr. Grumbloch said.

With great effort the man turned his head upon the pillow and stared at me with so penetrating a look, I was sure he knew me for the fraud I was, and I trembled.

"Not what I expected," he said. His voice was harsh,

and he paused between words as if he were catching his breath. "A thin little thing and peaked. You look half frightened to death." He turned to Mr. Grumbloch. "Thank you, Reginald." As I watched the solicitor leave, I wanted to run after him.

When we were alone, the grandfather, pausing between breaths, said, "I wanted just two things: to see you, Valerie, and to see the return of my own bird this spring, the bird I call *Hylocichla guttata pritchardi*. You are here, and as to the bird, I have no hope to hang on long enough for my little thrush." He heaved a great sigh. "The best I can hope for is that I may live to see the flycatchers' return, for they will soon be here."

For a moment I forgot my troubles, for the little fly-catchers that hopped about our garden were my favorites. "Do your flycatchers have long forked tails, like trains on ball gowns?" I asked.

"No, no. Forked tails to be sure, but short. Tell me what yours are like."

"Reddish on top with a black cap and tail feathers three or four times longer than their bodies. They're friendly, you know. They fly about me when I'm in the hammock." Suddenly I stopped, horrified. I had seen no hammock at the Pritchards'.

The grandfather noticed my hesitation. "What is it, child?"

I saw that he was having a more difficult time breathing.

Before I could stop myself I said, "I think you would be better with more pillows to raise you up a bit." Believing for a moment I was back in the hospital, I reached over and adjusted the pillows.

There was a silence, and I worried that I had gone too far. At last he said, "Yes, that is better." His look, sharp as an arrow, went right through me. "I've never known you to write a word about birds in your letters," he said. "Or anything else about the countryside down there, except to complain of the bugs and the heat."

Quickly I said, "It is hot and there are lots of bugs. We have to shake out our shoes each morning because of spiders and scorpions, but there are beetles as green as jade and wonderful bright-red dragonflies nearly as large as airplanes."

"You sound as if you liked Africa." He was staring at me.

I remembered I was Valerie and quickly said, "Oh, no. I couldn't wait to leave."

"Really? Well, you will have to tell me more about this country you dislike so much. I must rest now. Let me see you after your supper. But first come here for a moment."

Trembling, I crept close to him. He ran his hand over my hair and touched my cheek. I had thought his touch would be harsh, but it was gentle. "Not what I expected," he murmured, and closed his eyes.

Mr. Grumbloch had left. A young maid, who said her

name was Ellie, led me along the hall and into a bedroom very unlike the grandfather's, for this room was papered in a bright floral print, and the pale light of the February afternoon was streaming through two large windows. A fire glowed in the fireplace, warming the room.

Ellie's hair, which lay like two gold petals on either cheek, was fastened into a neat knot. She had wide-open blue eyes, as if she were astonished at everything she saw. "Here we are, Miss. I hope everything is suitable. Your grandfather had it all fixed up for you. There's a bath next door, and I've filled the tub with hot water. Your clothes are unpacked and tucked away in the drawers." Ellie was young, not yet twenty, I guessed. She said, "You have such pretty things, Miss. It was a pleasure to unpack them." She clasped her hand over her mouth. "I hope I haven't spoken out of turn, Miss." She put a serious look on her face and added, "You have only to ring if the fire needs tending to. Dinner will be at seven."

When she left, I looked about. There was a little desk with notepaper and pens laid out. A comfortable chair was drawn up to the fireplace. Books had been set out on a shelf; some of the titles, Dickens and Trollope, were my own favorites and had been a part of our modest library at home. Nothing could be cozier or more pleasant. For just a moment I was sorry I wasn't Valerie. How satisfying it would have been to have such a room for one's own. I allowed myself a little daydream. What if the grandfather did not die? What if he got better and I could live in the little room instead of an orphanage? Or if not that, perhaps he would let me work about the house like the young maid did. It was only a dream, for he would surely have me arrested as an imposter.

When I had had my bath, I put on yet one more of Valerie's dresses, and after wandering first in one wrong direction and then another, I found the stairway. Burker was waiting for me. Looking over his shoulder from time to time to be sure I had not wandered off, he led me to the dining room. As he seated me, I heard a slight groan as his crippled fingers lifted the weight of the massive wooden chair.

Burker disappeared. I sat alone at a long table that could have seated two dozen people. The young man who had taken our coats brought one course after another and then embarrassed me horribly by standing in the room while I ate. Once I tried to get him to leave. "Thank you very much, Arthur," I said. "I'll be quite all right alone."

He merely turned red and averted his eyes. He stuck to his place as if he were the last soldier standing to protect the fort. I saw that he was as anxious to leave as I was to have him go, but it was his duty to stay.

After dinner Burker said, "I believe your grandfather wishes to see you, Miss Valerie." He led me up the stairway and into the grandfather's room and then faded away, something he did very well.

"Well, my dear, are you comfortable?" the grandfather asked. His voice was stronger and his eyes brighter.

"Oh, yes. My room is so pretty."

He scowled, and the strands of red among his white whiskers seemed to glow like fire. In an angry voice he said, "I suppose I must ask how your parents are."

A longing grew in me to tell him the truth, but I worried at what the truth would do to him. What if upon hearing the news he threw up his hands and perished in front of me?

"My parents are very well," I said, and added under my breath, "and so they must be, for surely they are in heaven."

"Indeed." He frowned, his bushy eyebrows meeting over his nose. "I have just today had a letter from them saying that there was considerable expense in suiting you up for this trip, buying fancy dresses and so forth. They are asking for money." He stared at me.

Eagerly I suggested, "You could sell all those dresses and send the money to them." What a relief it would be to get rid of Valerie's hateful clothes, which it tortured me to put on.

"Sell them? You want new clothes? The latest fashion from London, I suppose. The African fashions are not good enough."

"Oh, no," I said. "I don't want any fashionable clothes. Just one dress that would be all my own."

His eyebrows shot up. "All your own? What in the world do you mean?"

I felt my cheeks burning. "I mean just one simple dress. Mother likes fashionable things, but I like plain things. I think they suit me better."

He stared quizzically at me for a bit and then said, "We'll take care of that by and by. Now, you will have to sing for your supper. My world has dwindled to just this room and this bed. Though I know you don't care for Africa, surely there must be one tale of the country you could tell me. I suppose there are lions and leopards and such?"

"Oh, yes," I said. I told him how in the nighttime you could hear the lions. "It is as if Africa itself were speaking." And then without thinking I began my story of the leopard and the duiker. I knew that Valerie would not have been walking about in the bush, so I said it had happened to a friend. I had not told the story to anyone before, so all the fear I had felt at that flash of menacing gold was fresh in my mind. As I told the story, my hands shook and my words rushed along as quickly as the leopard. When I had finished, I looked at the grandfather, and he was staring at me in a most alarming way.

"What a frightening story," he said. "You tell it as if it had happened to you."

Hastily I said, "Oh, no. It was my friend. My parents would never allow me to walk alone in the bush."

"Yes, I can quite see why. Who is this little friend of yours?"

"Her parents were missionaries and had a hospital." I stumbled over the words.

"I would not have thought my son would have much to do with missionaries. What was the girl's name?"

"Rachel Sheridan," I said, hearing my name spoken aloud for the first time in over a month.

The grandfather stared at me. "Well, Rachel must be an interesting child. I would like to hear more of her. Now I think I must rest. Is there anything you would like?"

"There is one thing. When I had my dinner, there was a young man who stayed in the room and watched me. It made me nervous."

"Oh, that is only Arthur, the new footman. He is just back from the war. Had a very bad time. He is the house-keeper Mrs. Bittery's nephew, and needed work. Best he could do, no other jobs available. He is probably more nervous than you are. Still, sitting alone in that great dining room won't do. I'll tell Mrs. Bittery you will be having your dinners up here with me."

"Thank you, Sir." I was not sure which would be worse, Arthur looming over my dinner or the grandfather with his sharp eyes watching my every move.

"And you are not to call me 'sir.' I am your grandfather. Now I am very tired, child."

As I tiptoed out, I could hear his faint snores.

Burker appeared as if by magic to announce, "There is a fire in the library, Miss." He saw my confusion and led me a slow, stately march to the library. There were shelves all the way around the room, and every shelf was crowded with books. I had not thought so many books existed. I thought how happy the beetles would have been with such a feast. There was a desk, several big leather chairs, a wooden floor covered with faded rugs, and in front of the fireplace a sofa with soft pillows. The shelves stopped several feet short of the ceiling, leaving room for a row of busts of what I imagined must be famous gentlemen. Lamps cast little pools of light in the room, and the sound and smell of the fire reminded me of the fires the Kikuyu would make outside their huts when they roasted goats.

Though the eyes of the famous gentlemen appeared to regard me with suspicion, I took a deep breath and picked out a book. It was Dickens's *Great Expectations*, which I had never read. I curled up on the sofa and after a few minutes forgot all my troubles and thought only of the troubles of Pip. I must have fallen asleep, for I was suddenly aware of whispers at the doorway.

"Children must have a bedtime," Mrs. Bittery was saying.

"Yes, but what is a suitable time?" Burker asked.

Mrs. Bittery approached me and cleared her throat. She was a plump woman whose softness was not unlike the couch pillows. Her face was round with small round eyes and a little pursed mouth. It was like the faces of people I had made when I first learned to draw. Her hair was braided and wrapped neatly around her head. She wore a long gray dress with a starched white collar and cuffs, and pinned to her waist was a set of keys. "Come along, Miss Valerie," she said. "I don't know what you have been used to in the jungle, but we keep early hours here."

She was so solemn that even in my misery I couldn't keep from mischief. "We go to bed early as well, but the roaring of the lions as they pace outside our windows keeps us awake."

She gave me a suspicious look and sent me off with Ellie.

When at last I was alone, I looked out across the snowy fields. The sky was bright with stars, but they were unfamiliar. The Southern Cross had been snatched from the sky. In all the darkness I could not see one familiar thing.

SEVEN

*I*n the morning I was awakened by something so welcome, I leaped out of bed and ran to the window. For a moment I thought I might be back at Tumaini. The sun was coming through the window, the first bit of sun I had seen in England. But it was still England. Ellie appeared to help me with my dressing. I wondered what Mother and Father would have made of having someone hand me shoes and stockings and fasten my dress. When I protested that I could do all that perfectly well, Ellie opened her eyes wider and, looking hurt, said, "I'm sure I'm trying my best, Miss," so I could only endure her help.

Then I asked, "Have you nothing better to do, Ellie?"

"You was why I was hired in the first place, Miss. If it wasn't for you, I'd be back home mucking out the stable and feeding the chickens. You was heaven-sent, Miss. I'm grateful, I'm sure. Your coming allowed me to better myself."

I wondered what Ellie would think if she knew feeding the chickens had been one of my jobs at Tumaini. "You lived on a farm then, Ellie?"

"Oh, that would be a fancy name for it, Miss. We had a plow horse and an old cow and the chickens I spoke of, but the bit of land is only big enough to feed us. We couldn't stay at all, but that Mr. Pritchard looks the other way when we can't meet the rent."

"He owns your farm?"

"Oh, he owns all the land hereabouts. And if you had to have a landlord, you couldn't have a better one. Will that be all, Miss?" She poked the fire into bright flames. "Breakfast will be waiting for you, Miss."

Burker guided me by slow, measured steps, making a kind of parade of two into the dining room, where a row of silver dishes held enough food to feed a village. "Arthur will assist you, Miss Valerie," Burker said, and disappeared. There was Arthur standing, red-faced, looking as if he would much rather face the German army. Nervously he lifted the cover of one silver dish after another.

"Who is going to eat all this?" I whispered to him.

He looked about as if he had been instructed not to speak to me and said in a low voice, "What you don't eat goes back to the kitchen, Miss."

"And in the kitchen?"

He shrugged. "We all have a turn, and what can't be saved goes to the pigs."

"It's a terrible waste."

He gave me a sidewise glance. "It is."

I settled at the place that had been set for me, and as I began to eat my breakfast, Arthur disappeared. I saw that the grandfather had ordered that I should eat in peace, though just then, as I sat alone at the table in the great dining room, Arthur would have been almost welcome.

After breakfast Mrs. Bittery led me to the grandfather's room. "He's waiting for you, Miss Valerie."

The grandfather was sitting up in bed watching the door. There was color in his cheeks, and his voice, which had been weak the day before, was imperious, truly Masai-like. "I hope you slept well, Valerie, for I have a task for you today if you are willing."

"Oh, yes," I said. I thought perhaps I was to sweep the stairs or make the beds, but I should have known better than to think I was to do something useful.

"I want you to be my eyes. It's the last day of February. The spring birds are due any day. I've made a list of three birds, what they look like, and where you might find them. You are to report any sightings back to me."

He handed me a list in a scrawly handwriting. Words had been crossed off and rewritten and letters retraced as though the grandfather had taken a great deal of time over the list and the writing of it had cost him much effort.

1. *Examine the beechwood tree at the entrance to the woods to see if the raven has made its nest there.*

2. *Look for a robin building its nest among the branches of the big oak tree by the fountain.*

3. *Keep an eye out for Hylocichla guttata pritchardi.*

When he saw the bewildered look on my face, he indicated a pile of books of various sizes, some as small as a folded handkerchief and some as large as a sofa pillow.

"The third book on the second pile, my dear. Page twenty-three, I believe. You will find a very good picture of a raven. Let me show you how it differs from a rook. The robin will be on page seventy-two, though this time of year the breast will be more sorrel than orange. Now for the *Hylocichla guttata pritchardi.* The Latin is quite simple. *Hylo* in a word means wood, and this little thrush is to be found near trees. *Gutta* refers to drops, or in this case the spots on the bird's chest. I'm afraid *pritchardi* is the result of my own vanity. When a new bird is found, it is often named after the person who discovers it, but the Royal Bird Society has refused to accept my bird as a new subspecies, and so they will not give it my name. They insist that I am mistaken in saying that it does not have the white eye ring, but I do not make mistakes where birds are concerned."

For a moment he looked almost ferocious, and then his voice softened and he said, "Little *Hylocichla guttata pritchardi* has a distinctive song. It sounds something like this. . . ."

Then came such a melodious whistle, I looked about thinking that a bird had flown into the room.

"Now you must try it so that you have it firmly in your head."

Over and over I copied as best I could the thrush's song.

"Off you go, my dear, and dress warmly. Ellie will find you some Wellingtons for your feet so you can tramp about and not worry about snow and mud."

Ellie slipped my feet into great rubber boots. Scarves and gloves were applied until I was so wrapped up, I could scarcely move. Still, as soon as I walked out into the cold English day, I found myself shivering again. With no idea where the beech tree might be, I approached a gentleman muttering to himself as he dug up a flower bed.

"You can't tell me the Lord made this clay—it's the work of the devil." When he noticed me, he said, "You'll be Mr. Pritchard's granddaughter, I suppose. From Africa I hear. That's the bottom of the world and hot. Too hot for proper flowers, no doubt."

I longed to tell him how my mother had tried for years to grow proper English flowers and could not for the very reason he gave. Instead I could only ask, "Please, Sir, could you tell me where the beech trees are?"

"No need to call me 'sir'—name's Duggen, diggen Duggen. Ha ha. The beech trees are over there, just where the woods start. Don't wander too far into them woods. I have no time to go looking for young ladies as gets lost."

I thanked him and headed for the beech trees, great high things with smooth gray trunks like the legs of elephants. A flock of rooks started up from one of the trees, but they hadn't the ravens' chin feathers the grandfather had described. I stood looking up into the bare branches. The wind crept up my sleeves and down my neck. I thought English birds foolish for coming into such cold country. Then I saw it, at first gliding overhead and then settling onto an arrangement of twigs that had been cobbled together and lay untidily on one of the branches. It was surely the raven.

With no help from Mr. Duggen I found the great oak tree by the fountain but no robin's nest. The walking about had warmed me, and the sun had melted the snow, and here and there I saw bits of green poking through the black earth. Though the fields were very different from the African bush, the feeling of space was the same. In all that open country I saw how small I was and how small my problems. I found enough room to begin to let go of my worries and fears. I would be the grandfather's eyes and ears, but somehow I would find a way to tell the truth as well.

It was nearly noon when Mr. Duggen discovered me listening to the thrush's song. Though I heard the song, I hadn't been able to see the bird. The song was so like the grandfather's imitation that I didn't know whether the bird was an enchanted man or the man was an enchanted bird.

"They've sent me to fetch you for your lunch," Mr. Duggen said. "They say you'll be frozen from head to toe. I told them fresh air never hurt a soul, but you best go in."

As soon as I had gulped down my meal of hot soup and a mutton chop, I ran up the stairs and hurried into the grandfather's room to make my report. The moment I opened the door, the words were out of my mouth. "I saw the raven, and it's started a nest, no robin, but I heard the thrush's song, only I couldn't see him."

"Well done. That is good news. To hear the excitement in your voice is almost as satisfying as being out there myself. Now come and sit next to me and tell me more about your Africa. You will be my living storybook."

After having to keep my secret for all those weeks on the boat, I longed to say aloud the names of the people and places I loved. "I could tell you about my friend Rachel," I said.

"And why this Rachel?" the grandfather asked. "Why not stories about yourself?"

"My life wasn't very interesting."

He gave me a quizzical smile. "Then by all means, let's hear about Rachel."

"She had an African friend, Kanoro, who taught her about the birds like you are teaching me. He taught her where to see the nightjars just as the sun went down and how to whistle like the mousebird."

"And can you whistle like a mousebird?" the grand-father asked.

"Oh, yes," I said, and began to purse my lips, for Kanoro had said he could not tell my whistle from a real mouse-bird. I stopped myself. Surely the real Valerie would not know how to make that whistle. I flushed. "That is, I think I once heard a mousebird but I don't remember now just what it sounded like."

The grandfather gave me a long look. "What did Rachel's missionary parents do?" he asked.

Here I thought I was on safe ground, for I was no longer talking about me but only my parents. "They had a hospital for sick Africans. It was too far for the Afri-cans in the bush to go all the way into Nairobi. It was a mission hospital, but because of the war there was no minister available, so Rachel's father, who was the doctor, did the preaching. Rachel used to help in the hos-pital."

"And doesn't she help there anymore?"

"Her father and mother died from the influenza." I took a deep breath and, sure I would be struck down by a thunderbolt, added, "Rachel died as well."

"You must have been very close to Rachel and her parents," the grandfather said. "There are tears in your eyes."

I clenched my fists until my nails bit into the palms of my hands. I blinked the tears away. "They were very good to me," I said.

The grandfather sank back upon his pillows and closed his eyes. "Thank you for the story," he said. "Now I must rest for a bit."

The grandfather's face was pale. His eyes fluttered shut. I tiptoed out of the room wondering if I had said something to worry the grandfather. I decided that I had better not talk of Rachel or her parents. It was too hard to keep my feelings from spilling over into the words.

After that I spoke only of the animals and the birds. Each day I was out on the grounds of the estate, and each evening I reported back to the grandfather a description of the birds I had seen. I had been at Stagsway a month when Burker, finding me on the stairway, handed me a letter. "This came for you, Miss Valerie."

At first I was startled, wondering who could know I was here, but a glance at the return address on the envelope sent me to my room, where I could open the letter by myself.

Dear Valerie,

We have had a cable from Mr. Grumbloch telling us that you have arrived at Stagsway safely. By the time you receive this letter, you will have become acquainted with your grandfather, and we hope you are in his good graces. The old gentleman has, I am sure, grown fond of you and will understand that it is difficult for you to be separated from your dear parents.

We are writing to him that we are so lonesome for you that we plan to visit England the end of the summer. Surely he must understand that it is natural for parents to wish to be with their only child. For your part you must do all you can to influence him in that direction.

Valerie, I am sure you realize that now that your grandfather has begun to care for you, it is more important than ever that you say or do nothing that might bring him sorrow, or hasten the end of his days.

With love,
Mother and Father

I had fallen into the Pritchards' trap. I had agreed to come to England for the sake of the old grandfather. That was what I had told myself. In my heart I knew that I had also hoped to escape the orphanage. Now the Pritchards planned to use me to help them to return to England. Once here, who knows what mischief they would do. I would tell the grandfather the first thing in the morning.

All night long I rehearsed my confession. I was resolved not to blame the Pritchards, for if I were honest with myself, I had to admit that I could have told the truth at any time. I could have confessed to Miss Limplinger on the boat. I could have told Mr. Grumbloch. It was my fault, and I would admit it. I believed that the grandfather was a kind man—hadn't Ellie said that he was a generous landlord? Yet I did not see how he could forgive me. My lie weighed so heavily on me, I could not wait until I told the truth.

At breakfast all the silver dishes were on display. Arthur was there to hand me a plate and take the covers off, but I was too upset to eat more than a bite of toast.

"Are you sick, then?" Arthur asked, and then blushed. "Sorry, Miss, I didn't mean to be nosy."

"That's all right, Arthur. I do feel a little funny today. I think I'll just go up to see my grandfather.

"I'm sorry, Miss, but Mrs. Bittery left word that your grandfather was not well and wasn't to be disturbed."

I was alarmed to hear that the grandfather was ill and upset that I had lost my chance finally to tell the truth. I did not see how I was to survive another minute with my secret. I put on my coat and went outdoors, for the great, dark, silent house was too much for me. Mr. Duggen had a wheelbarrow full of small, brightly colored flowers with large faces. When I asked what they were, he said, "Pansies, Miss. They don't mind the cold weather. I've seen them with snow on and none the worse for it. You might tell your grandfather I saw a willow wren this morning."

I was glad to have someone to talk with so that the time would pass. "Was Grandfather always interested in birds?" I asked.

"If you ask me, it started after his wife died and your father made all the trouble, if you'll forgive me. The old gentleman gave up on people and turned to birds. You can't go wrong there. They come and go just when they are supposed to. A bird won't disappoint you. I think one more disappointment would be the end of the old gentleman."

After that I wandered over toward the fountain. "One more disappointment would be the end of the old gentleman." The words were very terrible to me. How could I tell him the truth? I settled down on the fountain's ledge. With the water turned off the fountain looked forsaken. A bird flew out of the nearby oak tree with a bit of straw in its beak. I knew at once from its rusty breast that it was the robin. I hurried into the house, hoping that Grandfather was better and that the news of the robin's return would cheer him. Mrs. Bittery stopped me in the hallway outside Grandfather's room.

"You can't go in there now, Miss Valerie. Your grandfather sent for Mr. Grumbloch, and he's with your
grandfather right now."

A moment later Mr. Grumbloch himself appeared, a
scowl on his face, and swept by me, giving no return to my
greeting.

I crept down the stairs and huddled in the library, too
miserable to pick up a book. There on the desk was paper
and pen. I wrote a note:

> *Dear Grandfather,*
>   *Mr. Duggen saw a willow wren and I saw a
> robin. I hope you are feeling better.*
>   *Valerie*

I slipped it under the door of Grandfather's bedroom.
The next days were torture. Grandfather was too sick to
see me. I imagined the terrible Pritchards on their way.
I ate so little that the cook, Mrs. Nessel, came into the
dining room in her apron with a smudge of flour and a
stern look on her face.

"I am sure, Miss Valerie, that I am doing all I can to
give you tasty food. I suppose you are used to cooking
elephants and such, but I can assure you there are no elephants to be had at Butcher Brogan's."

"Oh, no," I said. "I've never had such good food. It's
just that I don't feel very well."

Her look softened. "I suppose you miss your parents. That's only natural."

"Yes," I said, glad to tell the truth for once. "I miss my parents."

Mr. Grumbloch returned, but the moment I saw him, I disappeared into my room, afraid of another of his angry looks. At supper I stuffed some of the food into my hand-kerchief and hid it in my pocket so that Mrs. Nessel should think I had eaten it and not be upset. I was so miserable, I was ready to leave Stagsway and walk wherever the road would take me. I had gone so far as to gather the few things that belonged to me and not Valerie and make a little bundle when Ellie appeared.

"Your grandfather wants you, Miss."

I knocked softly on his door and heard him summon me.

"Come and sit beside the bed, child; my voice is weak this evening." He looked at me for a long while. I thought, Now is the chance to tell the truth, but then I remembered Mr. Duggen saying, "One more disappointment would be the end of the old gentleman," and I swallowed my words.

"I have had a letter from my son," he said. "He and his wife wish to come to England. It seems they are lonesome for you and they wish for a reconciliation with me." He straightened up in bed, and I could imagine how he had once been an impressive and a stern man. "My son's reck-less behavior sent his mother to the grave. I can never forgive him for that. However, I have found that he has had his own disappointments. At any rate he has sent you. For that I can forgive him a great deal."

He paused to catch his breath. "It will be several months before they come, so we will have some time to welcome the spring and enjoy the summer. I had your note about the robin and the willow wren." He handed me a paper. "I have a new list. You can begin in the morning. Now I must rest."

I took the list to my room and read the names of the birds: swallow, turtledove, redstart. A description followed the name of each bird. I tried to sort everything out. Grandfather was not angry with me. The Pritchards would not arrive for several months. I did not dare risk Grandfather's life by revealing that the real Valerie was dead. I resolved I would spend the next months making Grandfather as happy as I could. As I made my resolution, I realized I no longer called him "the grandfather." Now, as if I were truly his grandchild, I called him Grandfather.

EIGHT

*A*s spring came on and the days warmed, I spent more and more time out of doors with Grandfather's lists. The fountain was turned on, and birds came to drink from it and bathe in its pool. The wagtails and whitethroats arrived, and the goldfinches turned yellow like bits of sun. Grandfather checked off a list he kept by his bedside and taught me the songs of the cuckoo and the nightingale.

"Bird by bird you have brought me the spring," he said.

Grandfather was able to leave his bed and sit in a chair by the window. When I was outside, I could look up and wave to him. He was eager to hear any news. I told him what flowers Duggen was planting and brought him bouquets of wildflowers, a little wilted and droopy from being crushed in my fist. Grandfather would name the flowers for me: cowslips, cuckooflower, and lords-and-ladies.

With the summer came foxgloves and forget-me-nots and cranesbill.

The English names made me remember Mother saying them over and how disappointed she was not to be able to grow English flowers in Africa. In the fields around Stagsway there were flowers everywhere you looked. Once I asked Duggen, "Why do you plant flowers when there are so many wildflowers?"

He answered impatiently, "They don't grow in neat rows, Miss Valerie, only ragged clumps here and there. What kind of garden would that be?"

Mr. Duggen carried on a battle with the ferrets and moles that dug up his garden, but he was fond of hedgehogs. "They're useful little things," he said. "They nibble the weeds." One day he showed me a baby hedgehog. It looked like a pincushion and was so tiny it fit into my hand. Its prickles were soft and its eyes still closed. "Will I make a cage for it?" Mr. Duggen asked.

I did not like animals in cages. I remembered a lion that a planter in Africa had kept caged as a kind of amusement. I shook my head. "Please put it back in its nest," I said.

In my wanderings over the summer I met the people who lived on Grandfather's estate and paid him rent for their cottages. There was Mr. Garth, who kept bees. I stayed at a distance as he put in the trays of comb that would soon be filled with honey. "Oh, Miss, you can come as close as you like. You couldn't ask for a friendlier bunch of bees." But I remembered the stings of the wild bees in Africa.

Many of the farmers grew hops for the making of beer, others grew nothing more than grain for their chickens and straw and oats for their horses. As I walked along the paths, the tenants would greet me and sometimes the mistress of the house would invite me in to see her children and have a cup of tea.

The cottage might be messy with tumbled beds, unswept floors, and grimy children, their mouths smeared with jam, their noses needing a good blow. More often the cottage would be tidy, the floor swept, the beds made, and the children scrubbed. Wherever I went, tea would be set out, weak tea where money was scarce. Plates of scones or biscuits where all was well, and thin slices of bread and butter where money was wanted.

Often the tenants would discuss their problems with me, knowing I would pass them along to Grandfather. "The chimney wants rebuilding," one tenant said. "It smokes so we daren't have a fire even to cook a meal."

I told Grandfather, and he issued an order to have the chimney repaired. When I reported sickness, he saw to it that Mrs. Bittery made up a basket of nourishing food and I would carry it to the sick tenant's cottage. Sometimes he sent his own doctor to check on an ill child or an elderly tenant. At times I recognized the illness and sometimes even suggested something to make the patient better, but I never mentioned my interference to Grandfather. Often the message I would carry from a tenant to Grandfather would be a plea for the wait of a month or two for rent. Grandfather would complain and talk of idleness and spendthrifts, but in the end he always agreed.

Again and again the tenants would tell me of neighboring landlords who threw their tenants out of their homes for any little thing, or landlords who charged exorbitant rents. "There aren't many like your grandfather," they said.

Bird by bird, flower by flower, tenant by tenant, I came to know and love Stagsway. Yet always in the back of my mind was Tumaini. Everything in England seemed pale and tame in comparison to Africa. The flowers and birds were not as colorful; no lion or leopard lay in wait in the fields, only a sheep and a cow or two. I missed the beating of the drums and the stories I used to hear in the Kikuyu *shamba*s. I missed the smell and the glow of the evening campfires and the sound of the lions at night. I missed the bustle and purpose of the hospital and the satisfaction of seeing patients carried sick and even dying into the hospital and then watching as the same patients left to return to their village, well and healthy again.

At the end of July I came upon a bit of Africa in Hampshire. I had seen birds with familiar names but different coloring; now I saw a bird that looked and sounded like birds I had known at Tumaini. I was in the orchard when suddenly a pair of hoopoes settled beneath one of the apple trees. They had the same cockade of feathers, tipped in black, sticking out of their heads as the African birds, and the same long, sharp bill. They had the same elegant walk. For a moment I thought I was seeing things, that I had imagined them because I wanted so much to be at Tumaini, but they were real. I stood there for nearly a half hour, not daring to move. The moment they flew away, I ran to Grandfather, bursting into his room. "Hoopoes!" I said. "I saw a pair of hoopoes. I am sure of it."

Grandfather was as excited as I was. He said, "I once heard a tale from Duggen's father, who worked here, of a pair of hoopoes. Tell Duggen no one is to go into the orchard to disturb them. What a sight we will have for Pernick." Mr. Pernick was the director of the Royal Bird Society. He called upon Grandfather each summer.

Grandfather said, "Now you must tell me about your African hoopoes."

"They are common in Africa. They were always about."

I was happy when Grandfather encouraged me to tell him not only of African birds but of all my memories of Africa. In the telling, it seemed I was back there once more. I told him of the lion that had carried away small children and how the lion had been hunted down and a mask made of his mane and a great *ngoma* held to both celebrate and mourn his death. Though the Africans feared the lions, they never questioned the lion's need to kill.

He asked about the illnesses that were treated in the hospital. "I suppose your little friend Rachel would tell you of such things," he said.

"Yes," I said, and described for him the terrible fevers and chills of malaria, and the children who suffered from worms, and how thorn wounds could become infected, and all the old people who were blind until their cataracts were removed. I told of the time there was a cholera epidemic and of the illnesses that came from bad water. "But there were never enough medicines," I said. "Everything had to be sent from England, and it took forever."

"Did the nurses come from England as well?"

"Oh, no, they were all Kikuyu. The nurses started in as sweepers in the hospital and the doctor would see which ones did the best work and who always came on time. Those were the ones he would train to become proper nurses."

"Rachel's father must have been an exceptional man," Grandfather said.

"Yes," I said, and turned my head so that he should not see my tears.

"And did Rachel's parents live in a large comfortable house like your parents?"

"Their house was made of mud-brick walls and an iron roof. The floor was earth that had been tamped down and covered with grass mats. The roof leaked when it rained. Kanoro would have to climb up on the roof and move the sheets of iron about."

"And wasn't such a life hard for your friend and her parents?"

"I don't think they thought much about it. Her father was too busy at the hospital and her mother had the school to attend to."

"And Rachel?"

"Well, she helped out at the hospital, but she was outdoors as well. She liked to visit the Africans' *shamba*s."

"*Shamba*s?"

I explained. "That's what we called the small African farms."

"Ah, I see. Like our lodges. And if Rachel were here, do you think she would go about to the lodges, taking tea and settling problems as you are doing?"

I was about to smile, taking Grandfather's remark as a little joke, but I saw that Grandfather was looking closely at me. Why was he comparing me with Rachel, pointing out how we were doing the same thing? I felt my face burning and could think of no easy answer.

He reached over and patted my hand. "I only meant that had I known her, I am sure I would have liked your Rachel. Now, tell me again how many tortoiseshell butterflies you saw on the rosebush this morning."

The end of August Mr. Pernick alighted. He was a

slight, slim young gentleman who, like his beloved birds, moved about so quickly and lightly, his feet seemed barely to touch the ground.

After introducing me, Grandfather said, "I have assured Pernick that you have seen and heard the *Hylocichla guttata pritchardi.* Your description could not be mistaken, and it matches mine to the last feather. There is no eye ring." He gave Mr. Pernick a severe look. "There can be no doubt that this is a new subspecies. It is high time it was adequately recognized." Grandfather turned to me. "Pernick and I are in the habit of going about together to see the birds," he said. "Since I can't accompany him this year, he will have the pleasure of your company, my dear. You are as familiar with the whereabouts of the birds at Stagsway as I am. I have also told him you have a special treat for him today."

Mr. Pernick was a lively companion. "Today is St. Bartholomew's day," he said. "It is said, 'Bartholomew brings the cold dew.' Autumn is on its way, and our friends the birds will soon be leaving us."

His words sent shivers up and down my spine, for I knew that like the cold dew, the Pritchards would soon arrive to make everything chilly. At that moment a grosbeak flew out of a rowan tree and Mr. Pernick caught at my sleeve in his delight.

Though we did a great deal of sneaking about among the trees, I could not find the *Hylocichla guttata pritchardi* for Mr. Pernick, but I assured him I had seen it. "Don't you think you could convince the Royal Bird Society to accept my grandfather's discovery of the bird? His heart is set on it."

"How I wish I could, Miss Pritchard, but science cannot do just what it wishes. If it could, we would all have a bird sporting our name. I promise that the proper committees are looking into it."

The words *proper committees* did not have a promising sound.

"Now, Miss Pritchard, what is this special treat you have for me?"

I led him to the apple orchard and, signaling him to be quiet, pointed to where I had seen the hoopoes. They were still there, hopping under the trees, pecking at the insects that buzzed about the fallen apples that lay rotting on the ground. We stood there frozen and silent until the hoopoes flew off.

"That must be the high point of my many visits to Stagsway. What a pleasure it has been to have you accompany me. What a treasure this place is, and how generous your grandfather is to promise it to the Royal Bird Society. I assure you we will treasure it. It will remain just as it is so that people may come from far and near to enjoy its beauty."

After Mr. Pernick left, having first said many kind things about me to Grandfather, Grandfather and I had a quiet dinner together in his room. The windows were open, and the curtains fluttered in the evening breeze. "Tell me, my dear," Grandfather said, "what do you think of my idea of giving Stagsway to the Royal Bird Society?"

"I think it's a fine idea, but what would happen to your tenants and to Mr. Duggen and the rest of the people who work for you?"

"That would all be taken care of. And what would you do if you were to have a great deal of money?"

Without thinking, I said the first thing that came into my mind. "I would find a way to rebuild the hospital at Tumaini."

"Yes," Grandfather said, "I believe you would."

NINE

*T*he Pritchards arrived in a chilly September rain. Grandfather had been cross all day. "What a miserable exchange," he complained. "All my birds leaving and my wastrel son and his wretched wife descending upon me. I told Grumbloch to keep them in the city, but they won't do as they are told. I won't have them here. They can pitch a tent outside." For all his complaining, Grandfather instructed Burker to ready a set of rooms for the Pritchards.

I hardly recognized the Pritchards. Gone was Mr. Pritchard's white suit and Mrs. Pritchard's flowered hat. Bundled up from head to toe in dark woolen cloaks, mufflers, gloves, and hats, they were complaining to Mr. Grumbloch as loudly about England as they had complained about Africa. In the vastness of the great hall, they didn't see me at first and began to load up poor Burker with their hats and scarfs and coats until the man nearly crumpled under his burden.

I wished that I could disappear, but Mr. Grumbloch said in a voice that seemed to be filled with irony, "There is your daughter."

At once they rushed at me. The two sides of Mrs. Pritchard's cloak fell over me like bat's wings, suffocating me. Mr. Pritchard nearly knocked me over in his haste to embrace me.

Mrs. Pritchard cried, "Valerie, dear, how we have missed our precious girl."

"We couldn't remain away from you for another day," Mr. Pritchard said.

I suffered their greetings and managed some few words of welcome, all the while noticing how Mr. Grumbloch stood aside and watched the Pritchards' performance. There were remarks on Mr. Pritchard's part about how pleased he was to be home again and on Mrs. Pritchard's part about how well I looked.

"I see that this life agrees with you, Valerie, dear," she said. "I suppose you are getting used to so comfortable a life." She gave me a quick, malicious look.

I could only nod my head and smile weakly. It was all I could do to keep from shouting that I was not their Valerie and had no wish to be. All the loathing I felt for them was turned against myself, for hadn't I let myself become a part of them? I had been led to believe Grandfather had

only a short time to live. I had thought my deception
would be for only a few weeks. But Grandfather was
stronger. Mrs. Bittery had said, "It's all your doing, Miss
Valerie. The old gentleman has something to live for now."
After hearing that, how could I tell Grandfather that I had
deceived him?

I suffered the Pritchards' embraces, saying little.

"We must go to Father at once," Mr. Pritchard said, but
Burker stopped him.

"I'm sorry, Sir, but your father is feeling unwell. He left
strict instructions that he was to see no one but Mr.
Grumbloch. I believe he looks forward to a visit with you
tomorrow morning."

"I don't understand," Mr. Pritchard said. "We have
come halfway around the world. Why is it that Mr.
Grumbloch is to see him and we are not?" For a moment
I thought he was going to rush up the stairway.

Mr. Grumbloch quickly said, "I have a bit of business
with him that will take no more than a moment."

Mr. Pritchard shrugged and turned away. He had
grown up at Stagsway, and in no time he was stamping
about up and down stairways and in and out of rooms.
While he was examining the house, Mrs. Pritchard took
me aside. She peered closely at me. I might have been
some odd species of beetle. Though no one could have
heard us, she asked in a hushed voice, "How often do you
see your grandfather?"

"Several times a day," I said. Had I known what was on her mind, I would have kept silent.

"And does he talk with you about Stagsway?"

"Oh, yes. We talk of it all the time. He depends upon me to tell him about the birds."

"I hope you haven't encouraged him in the wild scheme of leaving Stagsway to some bird association. Mr. Grumbloch told us all about it. Your grandfather must be out of his mind."

"Oh no," I said. "I think it's a perfect plan. Everyone will be able to come and enjoy the birds."

Mrs. Pritchard grabbed my arm. "You little fool. Why do you think we sent you here? To allow you to cheat my husband of his inheritance? Stagsway must come to him, and you must see that it does or you will find yourself locked away in a prison for impersonating our daughter."

I should have realized that it was an empty threat, for the Pritchards were surely as guilty of deception as I was, but I could think only of my own guilt and how saddened and miserable Grandfather would be to learn of their scheme and my part in it.

Little was said that evening at dinner, for Arthur was at his station while we ate. Mrs. Nessel had gone to a great deal of trouble over the meal. There was her special soup à la reine made with chicken and almonds; baked haddock, roast mutton, and apple tart. While Mr. Pritchard ate huge quantities, Mrs. Pritchard only picked at her food. For myself, I was too nervous to eat even a morsel and signaled Arthur to take away my plate before the untouched food was noticed.

Immediately after dinner the Pritchards made me accompany them into the library, where a fire had been laid and a tray of coffee set out. Burker poured out coffee for the Pritchards, and after handing it about with a shaking hand, he gave the fire some attention, groaning quietly as he straightened up.

The moment Burker was out of the room, Mrs. Pritchard said, "That man should have been dismissed years ago. He's much too old for the job. Aldon, you must find a butler for your father who will answer to us. The cook must go as well. The dinner tonight was inedible. The responsibility of managing this place is too much for your father. I'm sure he'll welcome our taking it over and sparing him the concern."

"It's not just the house," Mr. Pritchard said. "I had a talk with one of the tenants. Father is letting the lodges for a pittance. Rents must be raised. Of course, everything can't be accomplished in a day."

They had paid me no attention, but now I saw them looking at me.

"We'll see tomorrow, my dear, just how helpful you can be to us."

I was alone that evening in my room, once a place of happiness and safety, that now felt poisoned by the

Pritchards' greed and my own part in their scheme. I wanted to run away, but imagining Grandfather's face upon hearing such news, I quickly gave up the idea. I stood at the window staring out at the moonlit grounds, every inch of which I knew and loved. By the light of the moon I could see the bats darting about, hungry for rare fall insects. Soon they would fold their wings about their small bodies and hibernate for the winter. How I wished I could climb into some opening in a tree and curl up until the Pritchards left. How could I let the Pritchards make life miserable for Grandfather? Yet if I were suddenly to tell the truth, wouldn't that make him more unhappy? I pulled a blanket from the bed and put it around me. All night I sat up in the chair looking out the window at the grounds of Stagsway that had once seemed so friendly. The dark faded away, and a thin line of pink spread across the horizon. A few skylarks sang, but their song, which had always cheered me, seemed on this early morning the saddest I had ever heard.

When I dressed, I found my arm was bruised where Mrs. Pritchard had grabbed it, but the bruise was nothing compared to the injury the Pritchards had done me by entangling me in their evil scheme. Worst of all was my agreement to be a part of the scheme. Though I had told myself I had agreed out of concern for Grandfather, I knew I had let myself be talked into the deception. I had only myself to blame, and not the Pritchards.

At breakfast Mrs. Pritchard called Mrs. Nessel into the

dining room and announced to her, "I am sure you would welcome some suggestions regarding meals. After this you can submit your menus to me each morning, and I will go over them."

Mrs. Nessel bristled. "I've had no complaints from Mr. Pritchard," she said.

Mrs. Pritchard said, "Of course, my father-in-law is unwell and has not had the energy to see to such things."

I saw Mrs. Nessel tighten her lips to keep back an angry retort.

Before Mrs. Pritchard could say more, Burker announced that Grandfather wished to see us. The Pritchards ascended the stairs, and I lagged along.

Grandfather was sitting up in his chair, a scowl on his face, but he spoke gently to me. "Come here, child. Have you been out this morning?"

"No, Grandfather, but late last night I saw the bats, and just at dawn the skylarks were out."

He was quiet for a moment. "You must have been up very late and awake very early. I hope there is nothing to bother you." Grandfather turned to Mr. Pritchard. "Well, Son, so you have decided to pay me a visit."

I saw that Mr. Pritchard was intimidated by his father's piercing stare. "We were anxious to see you, Father, and of course we missed Valerie terribly. Now that we are here, we hope to relieve you of some of the responsibility of caring for Stagsway."

"Do you?" Grandfather asked in a cold voice. "That will be difficult to do from London."

"Oh, we wouldn't think of going to London," Mrs. Pritchard said. "We have no wish to leave you."

Grandfather stared at her. "I have had Mr. Grumbloch make arrangements for you to stay in London. There is a comfortable flat with every convenience. The car will take you today."

Mr. Pritchard's face went very red. "But Father, we have only just arrived. There are things that must be discussed."

"What things are those?"

I am sure Mr. Pritchard had not meant to rush at the subject so quickly but to lead up to it gradually, over a period of days. Now he saw there might not be another opportunity. "Mr. Grumbloch has told us that you mean to leave Stagsway to the Royal Bird Society. Surely that is foolish."

Grandfather turned to me. "Well, my dear, what do you say? Am I being foolish?"

The Pritchards were staring at me. Though she wasn't close enough to touch me, I could feel Mrs. Pritchard's hand cruelly squeezing my arm. I knew the Pritchards were anxious for me to discourage Grandfather's plan. They would surely punish me if I did not, but if I had deceived Grandfather once, I would not deceive him again. "I don't think you are foolish at all. I think it a fine idea," I said.

Grandfather turned to the Pritchards. "There you are. 'A fine idea'!"

Mr. Pritchard gave me a killing look. "Valerie is a child. What does she know of such things?"

With a smile Grandfather said, "I believe the Good Book says 'A little child shall lead them.'" He turned to me. "Your young friend Rachel, as the daughter of missionaries, would surely know that saying, would she not?"

The Pritchards went silent. Their faces were drained of color. They had no idea I had spoken of Rachel, nor did I understand why Grandfather mentioned her name now, but it had a terrible effect upon the Pritchards. They looked flattened, like two paper dolls, as if all the life had been pressed out of them.

Grandfather said, "Now I believe I will rest for a bit. As I said, Nivers will drive you to London as soon as possible." He rang for Burker.

"You are my father," Mr. Pritchard said. "Have you nothing more to say to me?"

"Only that should you wish to return to Africa, and I hope that you decide to do just that, I will gladly pay your fare."

"But we have no wish to return to Africa," Mrs. Pritchard said. "We despise it!"

"Then perhaps a little flat in London might be possible." Grandfather turned to me. "I am sure you will miss your parents, Valerie, so I will set you a task this afternoon to keep you occupied. The leaves are beginning to fall. Look up into the bare branches and see what nests you can discover and note their shape and size and how they are constructed. Later you and I will determine what birds built them. It will make a pleasant evening for the two of us."

The Pritchards were studying the way Grandfather spoke to me, which was kindness itself. Neither of us could hide how we had grown to care for each other. I saw the Pritchards exchange looks, and I sensed danger.

As Burker led us out, the Pritchards ordered me to follow them to their room. The moment we were alone and the door shut, Mr. Pritchard said, "Two things are plain. My father is very fond of you, and in spite of all we have done for you, you do not mean to use that fondness for our benefit. If we are to be sent away, you will come with us. Let us see how Father likes that. I daresay a few days without you will bring him to heel."

"I won't leave Grandfather," I said, surprising myself with my defiance.

"He is not your grandfather, and furthermore you have nothing to say about it," Mr. Pritchard told me. In a voice full of mockery he said, "Surely you wouldn't disobey your dear parents?"

Mrs. Pritchard stood over me as I packed, while Mr. Pritchard sent word to Grandfather that I was to accompany them to London. Only minutes later Burker came to tell us Grandfather wished to see me. Though he had not sent for them, the Pritchards accompanied me, determined not to let me out of their sight.

Grandfather gave me so searching a look, it was all I could do to keep from blurting out the truth.

"I understand you wish to go with your parents to London," Grandfather said.

I took a deep breath. "I would rather stay here, Sir."

"'Sir'? That's a cold word. Why not 'Grandfather,' as you always call me?"

Now was the moment for the truth, but before I could say a word, Mr. Pritchard spoke up. "I think, Father, that you of all people would say a child should obey her parents. Disobedience, I believe, is one of the crimes of which you once accused me. We must insist on Valerie's accompanying us. Of course, should you choose to welcome all of us here, then there would be no necessity for being parted from Valerie."

Grandfather drew himself up. "You will never be welcome here." With a final sad glance at me, Grandfather dismissed us.

With Burker supervising and Arthur doing the work, the car was loaded with the Pritchards' many suitcases and trunks. As we were getting into the car, Burker put his hand out to me. "We are sorry to see you leave, Miss Valerie." When his hand touched mine, I felt a piece of paper. As I withdrew my hand, I closed my fingers over the paper and slipped it into my pocket.

Moments later we were making our way down the drive, with its row of ancient oaks. I had decided on the truth. If I was to be taken from Grandfather anyhow, I now had no reason to hold back. I settled down and began rehearsing what I would say, only to find there were no suitable words, nor anyone to say them to. Miserable, I sank down in my seat, as far from the Pritchards as possible, and stared out of the window.

At any other time I would have been full of excitement at the thought of seeing the great city of London. Now every mile of the journey was painful, for it took me from Grandfather. The Pritchards had closed the glass window that separated us from Nivers and were making plans, talking as if I were not there.

"Any fool could see how the girl has ingratiated herself with my father," Mr. Pritchard said. "We sent her to assist us, and she has done nothing but assist herself, worming her way into the old man's affections."

"He'll come around," Mrs. Pritchard said. "To have the girl back, he must put up with us."

Just when I felt I could not endure another moment of breathing the same air as the Pritchards, we came to London. I had seen little of England, no more than Southampton and the country villages. When I thought of a city, I thought of Nairobi, with its two or three unpaved roads and its handful of government buildings and stores.

London was hundreds of streets and thousands of houses and stores. Cars and people were everywhere. I remembered Father reading a passage from the prophet Isaiah: "Woe unto them that join house to house, that lay field to field, till there be no place, that they may be placed alone in the midst of the earth!" Surely in such a city there would be no place where you could be alone. Now that I had resolved on the truth, I would have to find my way in this vast city, and there would be no one to guide me.

It was only when the Pritchards left me alone in my room, warning me not to leave it, that I was able to read the note Burker had slipped into my hand. It was from Grandfather, and folded into the paper was a pound note. I read: "If you need a friend, you must call upon Mr. Grumbloch in his chambers at Gray's Inn Square."

Our flat was on the ground floor. I could easily slip out the window as I once had done in Africa. I was both relieved and terrified. For months I had longed to tell the truth. But what would my punishment be? I quickly packed a suitcase, taking only what I believed I would need in a prison, for when I confessed to Mr. Grumbloch, that was surely where I would be sent. I had some idea that prisons were cold and damp, so I packed a sweater and heavy shoes and stockings; then I raised the window and climbed out into the great city.

TEN

*G*lad to have the suitcase to hang on to, I walked rapidly away from the flat and the Pritchards. As I hurried along, I saw how people raised their arms to hail a taxi. Taking a deep breath, I did the same. I was amazed to find that the simple gesture resulted in a taxi pulling up beside me. For a moment I forgot the difficulties ahead of me and felt the magic of my being able to bring a car to a halt. "Well, Miss," the taxi driver said, "now you've got me, speak up. Where are you headed?"

I read off Mr. Grumbloch's address.

"Gray's Inn, eh? A beehive of barristers. I'm glad it's you and not me that has to take up with the law. Off we go then."

I had hoped for an opportunity to arrange my words, but in no time we drew up in front of a huddle of brick buildings.

"That'll be a shilling and two pence."

I handed over my pound note and received in return a large handful of shillings and some pence from the driver. I was about to get out when the driver said, "I trust the ride was satisfactory, Miss."

"Oh, yes," I said.

"Well, then, since you are young and appear innocent in the ways of taxis, let me instruct you. It's customary to add a bit to the fare to show your satisfaction."

Ashamed of my ignorance, I gave the man a shilling.

"Well, that's handsome, Miss. Good day to you."

I stood with my suitcase looking at the tangle of buildings. Just as the taxi driver had said, it was like a beehive with dozens of corridors and doorways. A great number of men in black suits and white shirts were hurrying by like a herd of zebras. They gave me curious glances. A man in a uniform walked toward me. At first I thought he was a policeman, and for a terrible moment I believed he was there to arrest me, forgetting that I had not as yet confessed my crime. With relief I realized he was just a uniformed porter.

"Can I help you, Miss?" he asked, a friendly smile on his face so that I was no longer afraid of him.

I read off Mr. Grumbloch's address.

"Well, you've landed near port. That address is just over there. They'll tell you how to find your man." He noticed my suitcase. "You're sure you wouldn't be running away?" he asked.

"Oh, no, I have an appointment with Mr. Grumbloch."

He gave me a doubtful look and watched as I made my way to the building he had indicated. A man there pointed to a stairway. At the head of the stairs was a door on which was painted REGINALD GRUMBLOCH, BARRISTER. Now that the doorway was before me, I hesitated. It was not courage that made me walk through the door, but fear of the suspicious porter, who I knew would still be standing there watching to see what I did.

An elderly gentleman greeted me. He appeared not at all surprised to see me and amazed me by saying, "I believe Mr. Grumbloch is expecting you, Miss Pritchard." He led me through a room that appeared to be furnished with stacks and rolls of paper. He knocked briefly at an inner door, which he opened to reveal Mr. Grumbloch seated at a desk peering over a pile of paper so high, I could just see his eyes. I had rehearsed what I would say so many times that I had been sure I would not forget my little speech, but confronted with Mr. Grumbloch's perpetual frown and sharp blue eyes, I could only conjure up three words: "I'm not Valerie."

I was resolved not to give way to tears or to otherwise appeal for pity but to accept my punishment. "You can put me in prison," I said. "I've brought warm clothes."

"Well, Rachel," he said, and I jumped to hear my name, "you had better sit down and tell me the whole story." He pulled out a chair and took my suitcase from me.

Astounded, I managed to stutter, "Why do you call me Rachel?"

"That is your name, is it not?"

"Yes," I whispered, "but how did you know?"

"Your grandfather and I knew almost from the beginning. He could not believe that you were the same Valerie who had sent him letters full of wheedling requests for money and whining complaints about Africa. The stories you told about Rachel were told with all the feeling of someone telling her own story. At your grandfather's direction, I contacted the mission board. Over the years your parents had sent them pictures of Tumaini, and you were in some of the pictures. Of course the mission board was under the impression that you had perished with your parents.

"When we learned of the many deaths from influenza, we guessed what had happened to Valerie and why the Pritchards had sent you in her place. I explained to the mission board that you were well taken care of and, for the present, quite happy where you were. Was I wrong in that?"

"Oh, no. But why didn't you and Grandfather say something?"

"I was all for sending you packing, but your grandfather was curious at first and then grew very fond of you. He believed you would tell us the truth one day. I must say I was not so sure. I am pleased to see that he was the better judge of your character."

"I won't go to prison?"

"Indeed not. Your grandfather's orders are to return you to Stagsway at once, unless, of course, you wish to remain with the Pritchards."

"I never want to see the Pritchards again, but what will I do at Stagsway?" I think I had some idea that I would be put to work in the scullery, or perhaps, I thought with a little hope, I might help Mr. Duggen. Whatever my task, how grateful I would be to return to Stagsway.

"You will do just what you have always done. You will be a companion and comfort to your grandfather."

"But he's not my grandfather."

"I believe we can do something about that. Now, you had best begin at the beginning and tell me what led you to impersonate Valerie."

I had been so anxious for so many months to tell my story, the words came pouring out: my love of Tumaini and my work there in the hospital and all the people Father cured and Mother's school. I told about the influenza, my parents' death, the fear of the orphanage where they had grown up, the Pritchards' convincing me that Grandfather was near death and that I would be saving his life. I said they had tried to make me help them take over Stagsway. "I could never let them do that. Grandfather is stronger now, and I had to tell the truth.

"But Mr. Grumbloch, I don't believe I could face Grandfather. If I'm not to go to prison, I had better be sent to the mission orphanage."

"What, and make your grandfather miserable? No, indeed. I am a bachelor with no suitable lodgings for you, but I will phone my sister, Frieda. You can stay with her tonight. Tomorrow I will drive you back to Stagsway, but first we must face the Pritchards."

"Oh, no," I pleaded. "I couldn't."

Mr. Grumbloch's frown returned. He had been speaking gently to me; now he made his voice very firm. "They must be apprised of your whereabouts." He put his hand on mine. "I will be there to support you."

I knew that I must face the Pritchards—that if I could not stand up to them, I would always think of myself as weak.

The Pritchards appeared shocked to see me. I realized that they still believed I was in my room. That I should appear with Mr. Grumbloch made no sense to them at all. They stood side by side at the entrance to the flat, too confused to invite us in. Finally Mr. Pritchard stood aside, allowing us to walk into their sitting room.

"Valerie," he said, "I don't understand. What are you doing with your hat and coat on? Why is Mr. Grumbloch here? You had better go to your room. We have things to discuss with Mr. Grumbloch."

"I believe, sir, that Rachel has something she wishes to

say to you." Mr. Grumbloch gave me a gentle push forward.

At the sound of my name the Pritchards drew close to each other, so that I had to face a solid wall of fury. "What do you mean, 'Rachel'? That's not her name." There was no conviction in Mr. Pritchard's voice.

"It was as much my fault as yours," I said. "I'm very sorry if I have made trouble for anyone. I only meant to make Grandfather happy and escape the orphanage. After I got to Stagsway, I didn't know how to tell the truth."

In a weak voice Mr. Pritchard said, "She doesn't know what she is saying."

"She knows exactly what she is saying," Mr. Grumbloch said. "Your father wishes me to tell you that he is very sorry for Valerie's death. Though he didn't know her, still she was his granddaughter and he mourns her. Further, he is in your debt for bringing Rachel into his life. Therefore he will try to do his Christian duty and forgive you. But he is not prepared to go so far as to have anything to do with you. He will give you an allowance that will allow you to live here in England if you wish, but the moment you attempt to set foot in Stagsway, or to contact him or Rachel, the allowance will be withdrawn."

Mrs. Pritchard had gotten over her shock and was shaking with anger. "You little fool," she spat at me. "You outsmarted us. You mean to have Stagsway and all the old man's money for yourself."

I felt as if she had struck me. "No," I said. "I want nothing for myself. I only want Grandfather to be well and happy."

Mr. Grumbloch took my hand. "I am not surprised, madam, that you would accuse Rachel of the very thing you are guilty of yourself. We are leaving now. Any further business will be done through me. Do no forget the condition of your allowance. You are not to bother your father or Rachel—not one letter, not one word." With that we left.

Mr. Grumbloch directed the taxi driver to Gordon Square. I was still trembling as Mr. Grumbloch led me up the walk to a narrow brick house. He cautioned me, "Though sensible in her own way, my sister is inclined to be somewhat impetuous and is, I'm afraid, a little too involved with art and other nonsense."

Miss Grumbloch was there to greet us. How different she was from her brother. He was as firm and rigid as a stone, while his sister with her dress of silken gauze and her hair loose about her shoulders was as airy as a cloud of mist. From the moment she opened the door to us, Frieda Grumbloch was kindness itself.

"My dear," she said when she saw me, "how pale you are." She took my hands in hers. "You are cold as the grave. Come into my sitting room, where there is a warm fire. I'm sure my brother has not thought to feed you. I'll have Effie bring you a nice hot cup of tea and some lovely biscuits from an enchanting shop I just discovered."

Mr. Grumbloch said, "I will leave Rachel to your care, Frieda. I must get back to business. I will be here to pick her up first thing in the morning."

We were soon settled in front of the fire. At first I was afraid to pick up the cup of tea, for my hands were still shaking, but Frieda—she had insisted I call her that—was so kind, and the room in which I found myself so unusual, I felt some of my worry melt away. One wall of the room was painted with a scene of trees and flowers. The lamp-shades were of bits of colored glass, put together to look like flowering trees. Even the window draperies and the rugs were woven into patterns of branches. I felt as if I had settled in an enchanted forest. Frieda herself, with her flowing hair and trailing skirts, looked like a wood nymph.

She saw me looking about the room. "The mural on my wall was painted by a friend," Frieda said. "The draperies are my own poor effort. Later I'll show you my loom. Now, Rachel, we must talk about you. My brother has told me your story. What a time you have had."

"What I did was very bad."

"You fell among evil people at a time when you were most in need of help," Frieda said. "Now you are rid of them and you can be yourself."

"I don't see how Grandfather can ever forgive me."

"I can assure you that he has. My brother says your

grandfather wants nothing more than to have you with him for as many years as he has left to him. Are you not happy at Stagsway?"

"Oh, yes. I've never been happier." But that was not true, and I was resolved that from now on I would speak only the truth. "I was happier with my parents at Tumaini, but I can never go back to that."

"Is it just your parents that you miss? Or do you miss Africa and your friends there as well?"

I could not keep the tears from my eyes.

"I see," she said. "Tell me what it was like."

I told her the story I had told to Mr. Grumbloch. "There is no hospital and no school now," I said. "All my mother and father's work at Tumaini was for nothing."

"Surely not. Think of all those they made well and all the children who have the gift of reading and writing. All that they accomplished will be built upon. Now you must rest for a bit."

Though I did not think I could close my eyes, my lack of sleep the night before overcame me, and the moment I lay down, I was asleep. It was dark when I awoke. Frieda had prepared a little evening feast, which we had in a cozy way in front of the fire. Our talk turned to books, and she asked what I had read. "Excellent, excellent," she said, "but you would have found nothing recent in your grand-father's library. If you love books, I will give you some to take with you, and one day I will introduce you to the writers of the books. With a mind as bright as yours you will want to find a proper school to continue your education."

"You mean leave Stagsway and Grandfather?"

"Though I am sure your grandfather will be reluctant to part with you, you must go to school. You must continue the education your mother began. Young women must have an education. You would be away only for the school term. You will be at Stagsway on your vacations and, of course, for the summers. I believe I know of just the right school. Now you have listened to me chatter long enough. We'll get you settled in your room. This has been a long day for you."

While I was in bed that night, the thought of going away to a school kept me awake. As much as I hated to think of it, I knew that one day Grandfather would not be there. I would have to find some life for myself. Much as I loved Stagsway, I did not think I would be happy living there alone with only the birds for company. But the only dream I had was of Tumaini and the hospital, and that was an impossible dream.

When I set off for Stagsway with Mr. Grumbloch the next morning, along with a packet of books, I carried a letter Frieda had written to Grandfather. As Frieda saw us off, she said, "Remember, Rachel, if you ever have need of someone to talk with, you must come to me."

It was on the way to Stagsway that Mr. Grumbloch

showed me the papers he had drawn up on Grandfather's orders. They were adoption papers with my new name, Rachel Pritchard. I knew then that Grandfather had forgiven me and that I would have a home, but something inside me was sorry that once again I would lose Rachel Sheridan.

BOOK THREE

Rachel Pritchard

ELEVEN

I flew up the stairway to Grandfather's room, and bursting through the door, I fell on my knees next to his chair. In no time we were hurrying to tell each other all the things we had not been able to say. We talked long into the night. I told Grandfather, year by year, month by month, almost day by day all the stories of Tumaini.

Grandfather told me how Mr. Pritchard, after his brother's death, had gambled away thousands of pounds. When Grandfather had refused to give him more money, he had stolen it from the estate, and the shame of the theft had made his mother so miserable, she had become ill. "It was then I sent him off to Africa. I couldn't bear to have him by me. When I began to see in Valerie's letters the same greediness for money, I hoped by bringing her here I might spare her repeating her father's mistakes. It was not to be. But I have you, and for that I am most grateful."

"How did you guess that I was Rachel?" I asked.

"You gave yourself away almost from the first by talk-ing about your 'friend' Rachel and the hospital and the land. I could see the longing in your eyes. Out of curiosity I had Grumbloch contact the mission. I believe my curios-ity kept me alive in those weeks. I could not die until I had solved the mystery. As soon as he saw the pictures of you and your family, we knew. By then I had come to love you, and I felt sure that when you were ready, you would tell me the truth. I am very sorry for the death of my grandchild, but you are a great gift. I believe Mr. Grumbloch has told you that I mean to adopt you. I hope that will please you."

Seeing the look of pleasure on Grandfather's face, I could not tell him of the small doubt I had about losing Rachel Sheridan, I only took his hand in mine, saying that nothing would please me more. As soon as I said it, I thought how I had resolved to say nothing but the truth and how already I had fallen short of my resolve. I saw that truth was very complicated.

When Ellie came to help me to get ready for bed, she stared at me as if she could not quite believe what she was seeing. "Oh, Miss Valerie, I mean, Miss Rachel. We was talking below stairs. It was so exciting, your not being who you were and your real life so different and all. It must be a bit like it is for me. At home on the farm there's a bath every once in a while because of the trouble of getting the tub out and heating the water and all. Here Mrs. Bittery makes me wash every day until I'm sure my skin will come off."

"Oh, Ellie," I said, smiling. "That is just how it was for me." I could not help wondering how many people like Ellie and me were not always who they pretended to be.

That night I slept once more in the room I had come to love. I tried not to worry about Frieda's insistence on my going away to school. I would have been content to stay at Stagsway and make Grandfather happy, but I had made the journey all the way from Africa, and the school would not be so far.

The next morning Grandfather sent me out to see if the house martins had left.

"The house martins are gone," I reported, "and the witch hazel is blooming." I had seen the spidery yellow blossoms standing out on the bare branches.

"The martins gone and the witch hazel blooming. Autumn is truly here and you must follow the swallows, Rachel."

I stared at him. In the joy of being out of doors again, I had forgotten all about school and wondered if I was to be sent away after all.

"In her letter to me Miss Grumbloch pointed out that you have had no schooling since you came here. Your mother, who was at such pains to teach you, would surely have wanted you to continue your education. We must find a proper school for you."

"Must I leave?"

"It would be selfish of me to keep you to myself. It isn't just the schooling, important as that is; you must have friends your own age."

By the end of the month I was enrolled in a boarding school, Ditchley. It was in Sussex, not too far from Stagsway, so that I could easily come home during vacations. Still, I worried. "I've never gone to a proper school," I told Grandfather. "I've never had girl friends. I won't know how to act."

"Nonsense, my dear. You are a very bright child, and your mother made a fine job out of her teaching. I have seen you tackle books from my library that would puzzle a university student. As for things like numbers and science, girls needn't worry about such things."

At the end of October I said good-bye to Grandfather and left for Ditchley. Nivers drove me in the car with my luggage and a basket from Mrs. Nessel packed with biscuits and cakes and her homemade jams and jellies.

With no thought of my dignity I climbed up on the backseat so that I could have the last possible look at Stagsway. When it was out of sight, it was all I could do to keep from jumping out of the car and running back. It seemed that my whole life was spent leaving the places I loved.

My idea of school was Mother and myself under a tree with our books, or Mother with her pupils grouped about her. There the schoolhouse walls were made of grass mats, which let in the sun. The roof was open to the sky. Ditchley was a large stone building with a slate roof. I felt I was entering a prison. In Tumaini the pupils ran in and out as they liked; at Ditchley we marched in lines from class to class. Every minute of our time was taken from us and squeezed into a schedule that had nothing to do with our wishes.

On my first day at school, Miss Ethelward, the headmistress, took me into her office. She peered at me from glasses pinched onto her nose. Her hair was pulled back into a skimpy knot. Her clothes were a dull gray, and her shoes so heavy, I wondered at the effort it took to lift one foot up after the other. Yet in spite of her severe look and her stern manner, I noticed that a teddy bear sat on her desk with a pink ribbon around its neck.

"There can be no learning without discipline," she said. "We do not believe in discipline for discipline's sake here, only discipline for learning's sake. Now, what languages do you know? Latin, of course. Greek? French?"

"Swahili," I said, "and some Kikuyu and a few words in the Masai language."

"Good heavens! No Latin!" She could not have been more amazed had I said I had not learned to breathe.

"I know three Latin words," I said. "*Hylocichla guttata pritchardi*."

There were more pained looks when Miss Ethelward

learned of my difficulties in arithmetic. With little hope in her voice, she asked, "What books have you read? If, indeed, you have read any books at all."

At last I had something to say. I had made good use of Grandfather's library. Out tumbled my favorites. "Everything of Jane Austen, *Wuthering Heights*, and *Jane Eyre*, and all of Dickens and Shakespeare's plays except *Coriolanus*, because everyone kills everyone, but I know *Midsummer Night's Dream* almost by heart. Wordsworth is my favorite poet, but Browning tells such wonderful stories, and Byron . . ."

Miss Ethelward raised her hands as if she were warding off a swarm of bees. I saw that she was smiling, but immediately the smile disappeared as if she had been caught at some forbidden activity. "I can see that you are a special problem, but discipline will solve any little difficulties."

I was soon floundering about in the deep waters of mathematics and Latin verbs, but it was the discipline that sank me. At Tumaini I had been free to go where I wished. At Stagsway, when I was not with Grandfather, I roamed where I liked. At Ditchley no minute of my day belonged to me. We rose at seven, washed in cold water, put on our uniforms, breakfasted on gluey porridge, bread and margarine, and weak tea, and after a brief stop at chapel were in our classroom seats by eight o'clock. Even our recreation was scheduled. There was no time to look for birds or wander into the nearby woods. We were put into teams and sent into violent pursuit of a helpless ball.

Not everyone followed the schedule or worked as hard at their lessons as I did. Some of the students did not mind coming unprepared to class. They behaved like lapwings. When you get close to a lapwing's nest, the little bird makes a great commotion to lead you away so you won't notice its young. When our history teacher, Miss Edgar, asked Sarah Evans for the date of the Battle of La Hogue, Sarah had a terrible coughing fit and had to be excused to drink some water. When Elizabeth Weston could not explain why England had a civil war in 1642, she began to scream, saying she had seen a black widow spider in her desk. The girls were often mischievous, but I didn't dare misbehave. Unlike me, the other girls had never in all their lives done anything really bad. In pretending to be Valerie, I had already used up all my wickedness.

I looked forward to making friends at school, but I had come late and friendships had already been formed. I could not find my way into their world. They seemed to have a secret code I couldn't decipher. They talked about their horses and shopping in London for clothes and dances and boys they knew. Several of the girls had had French governesses when they were growing up, and their conversation was sprinkled with French words I didn't understand. I knew when I was with them they used French to talk about me. It was considered bad form to speak of the books you read. I loved the Greek plays, which were so beautifully tragic, and longed to know what they sounded like in Greek. When I asked one of the girls who was studying Greek to read me a line or two, she gave me a withering look. Later I saw her and another girl looking my way and giggling. I heard the words *gauche* and *ingénue*.

There was some interest in me when it was learned that I had lived in Africa, but my dismal performance in class, and then my resolve to work hard and improve, did nothing to help me make friends. If I made an error, some girl was sure to whisper, "That's how it's done in Africa."

Somehow the other girls had discovered that my parents were missionaries who had died in Africa. I walked into Latin class one morning to find on the blackboard a picture of my parents in a kettle over a fire with horrid caricatures of Africans dancing around the fire. The stupidity and cruelness were too much for me, and I ran out of the room in tears and right into Miss Ethelward, who marched me back into the classroom.

"I think it is time you learned what Rachel's parents did in Africa. Rachel, I want you to describe the hospital at Tumaini and the people who worked there."

There were groans from the girls. At first I could hardly get a word out, but then my anger took over and I described the women who would have suffered from complications of childbirth had there been no hospital and the man whose appendix might have burst and who would have died had my father not been there to operate. I told them how our nurses and Father's assistant were Africans. "They don't boil missionaries," I told them, my face red with anger. "They save lives and they are a whole lot smarter than the stupid, silly girls who drew that picture." There wasn't a sound in the room. The girls were all looking down at their desks.

"Thank you, Rachel," Miss Ethelward said. "That was very instructive, although you would have done well to omit your last words. What one says in anger is seldom worth saying." Still, for just a moment I saw that fleeting smile that Miss Ethelward guarded so carefully.

That afternoon Nora stopped me on my way into the dining hall. "Do you want to sit with me?" she asked. "Pay no attention to those fools—they're incredibly dense." Nora was Irish. Her father had something to do with the Irish government and was stationed in England. Nora was slim with black curls, eyes the color of violets, and a love for words. She could say whole poems by heart.

Nora and I became friends. She took it upon herself to explain everything to me: the other girls ("They're like a school of fish all swimming in the same direction"), the school ("You get your money's worth"), and the way of the world in general ("You have to give as good as you get"). What really made us friends was her love of Shakespeare, but where I read it, she acted it. Her favorite scene was from *Hamlet* where it says "Enter Ophelia, distracted."

Nora went around reciting Ophelia's words, "White his shroud as the mountain snow," as if she were truly mad.

After the Christmas vacation the winter inched along and I had only my letters from Grandfather and the thought of Easter vacation to cheer me. In March Grandfather's letters began to speak of spring. "Mr. Duggen has reported seeing the willow wren, and from my window I have noted the swallows returning from your Africa. The other night I heard the nightingale."

At last the term was over. Grandfather was not well enough to come down for Prize Day, but Frieda came. She arrived in a flurry of bright scarves, sweeping skirts, and a hat that had more flowers than Mr. Duggen's garden. Against the dull gray classrooms and the gray school uniforms, Frieda was as colorful as the showiest African bird. She sat with the parents during assembly and applauded enthusiastically when I received the literature prize, a volume of Byron's poems.

Grandfather had sent Nivers and the car to bring me to Stagsway. Frieda was on her way to visit friends in Hampshire and was to ride part of the way with us. I shook Miss Ethelward's hand, promised to write to Nora, and burst out of school as out of a prison.

Nivers loaded my trunk and settled us in the car. Once we were in the countryside, I breathed a great sigh of relief. Bluebells covered the fields so you could hardly tell sky from earth. The hawthorns were garlanded with white blossoms, and the golden chain trees hung with clusters of yellow flowers. The whole world was a flower shop.

"Rachel," Frieda said, "there is something I must tell you. I have been to the mission society."

For a moment I was afraid I was to be sent to the orphanage after all. "Is Grandfather unhappy about my schoolwork?"

"On the contrary. Miss Ethelward has written him, and he is pleased at how well you have done, though I suppose if he had had his way you would not have gone to school at all."

"I wish he had had his way."

"Do you really wish that, Rachel? If you have a good head on your shoulders, why shouldn't you use it? You have Stagsway now, but your grandfather is not well, and one day the estate will belong to the Royal Bird Society. What will you do then? Would you be happy in a flat in London?"

"Oh, no." I could not keep myself from blurting out, "I'd find a way to go back to Tumaini."

"I thought so. It's why I went to the mission society. You told me how unhappy you were that the hospital has been closed. Unfortunately I was told by the society that the hospital at Tumaini is not a priority for the society. They have other missions that they feel have greater needs, and there is a shortage of doctors just now. 'Perhaps one day when a doctor is trained,' they said."

I shook my head. "It's hopeless. They'll never find a doctor. I'd have to turn myself into one before they agreed to reopen Tumaini."

"Could you do that?"

I stared at her. When I had uttered the words, I had not taken then seriously, but now I asked myself, "Why shouldn't I be a doctor?" My heart was pounding; my thoughts flew everywhere. All these months I had told myself that I would never see Tumaini again. Now there might be a way. I asked, "Frieda, is there such a thing as a woman doctor?"

"Yes, indeed. Women are certainly training to be doctors. There is even a school for women doctors."

I thought of what was ahead of me: three more years of Ditchley and then medical school. It seemed impossible, yet I knew something of hospitals and doctoring, and against expectations I had done well in science at school. "What would Grandfather say?"

Frieda shook her head. "It would be best if you said nothing about this to your grandfather for the time being. Like my dear brother, your grandfather is not a modern man. He might not understand a woman wanting to be a doctor."

"I couldn't deceive him again."

"I don't suggest you deceive him. We all have secrets in our hearts. That will be your secret. It will take nothing from your grandfather, and the idea of it will help you to endure school, and to do well there."

At first I thought my idea of becoming a doctor was an impossible dream. The doctor who cared for Grandfather was a towering, gruff, elderly man with a beard and a commanding voice. I was a young, stupid girl who could barely manage a simple Latin sentence, much less pronounce the fearsome Latin names of diseases. But the longing to return to Tumaini was strong. If learning to be a doctor would make it possible, I would learn to be a doctor if it killed me.

TWELVE

*S*ummer had come to Stagsway. The rooks had built their nests, and already their young were hungry for crawly things. I pushed my dream of returning to Tumaini to one side, though I devoured all the scientific books I could find in Grandfather's library and Frieda gave me a book about Marie Curie's discovery of radium. I tried to improve my Latin and kept a list of irregular verbs in my pocket. While gathering raspberries for Mrs. Nessel, I frightened the grosbeaks from the brambles with my conjugating. I spent long days wandering over the grounds taking notes for Grandfather, who was putting the final touches on his inventory of all the birds that had been seen at Stagsway. He was delighted when I reported a Dartford warbler, a rare bird, seen only once before at Stagsway and that time by Grandfather himself when he was a young man. And always he asked about *Hylocichla* *guttata pritchardi.* He was still sending letters to Mr. Pernick, but as yet the Royal Bird Society was not convinced. At Mr. Pernick's suggestion I began to keep my own diary and description of the little thrush. "It may be," Mr. Pernick said, "that a second set of observations will help convince the society."

As the crow flies we were close to the sea, and there was always the excitement of some seabird wandering off its course. Herring gulls came often and once I saw a puffin, but the most exciting day came toward summer's end. Stagsway was on the edge of the New Forest, an ancient woods where William the Conqueror once hunted and where his two sons were killed, one prince by a stag and one by an arrow. There were thousands of acres of fields and trees, with beeches and oaks so large my arms wouldn't stretch a quarter way around them. There were tiny, hidden streams where I took off my shoes and cooled myself on hot days. Sometimes I had a lunch of cheese and apples I had stuffed into my pockets along with the Latin verbs. Loosestrife and grass-of-parnassus and bog myrtle grew along the rivulets, and dragonflies and hummingbirds buzzed around me. There were fields of heather visited by tortoiseshell and red admiral butterflies. In the deserted parts of the New Forest I could almost feel I was back in the bush around Tumaini.

One day, walking through the heather, I came upon a wild pony. My heart stood still. I knew there were hundreds of wild ponies in the New Forest. I had seen them trotting along in the villages or stretching their necks over a fence to graze on someone's flower bed, but a wild pony nibbling a flower in a village is not the same as coming face-to-face with one all alone in a deserted field. I don't know which of us was the more surprised. It was plump, well-fed, and all white except for a reddish brown mane. Its ears were twitching, and it gazed at me coyly from under its forelock. I dug an apple out of my pocket and held it out. After a minute it extended its neck gracefully and plucked the apple from my hand with its soft lips. A moment later it was cantering away across the field, and though I had seen it for only a few minutes, I felt a terrible loss at its leaving. I don't know what it was, but there was something about the ghostly pony's appearance that reminded me of Valerie, as if she had come to tell me she had forgiven me for taking her place. I was pleased thinking of her carefree and happy.

I came to the same spot every day. Some days the pony was there and other days, though I waited, it never appeared. Mrs. Nessel remarked about all the apples and carrots that were disappearing from the storage room, but I never mentioned the pony, not even to Grandfather. Something in the wildness of the pony, something in its independence, attracted me. It was as if Valerie had a message for me. The wild pony did as it liked, went where it wished; why shouldn't I?

Once when Grandfather spoke of my schooling being over in three years, I said, "Then would I go to university?"

"Whatever for? You have books in the library if you have a mind for that kind of thing. It's not healthy to be shut up inside."

"There's so much I don't know. Languages and history and science."

"Nonsense. That's all very well for a scholar or a man who has to make his way in the world, but you will be well provided for. You have no need to lift a finger."

"I wouldn't want to be useless all my life."

"Useless! I should think not. You have shown a great aptness for the scientific study of birds. When the society moves here, you will be of the greatest importance."

Much as I loved the birds of Stagsway, I did not want to spend the rest of my days in their study. I shuddered to think that the only thing I would have to look forward to would be long walks with Mr. Pernick. Before I could stop myself I said, "Women are doing all sorts of things; they are even becoming doctors."

"Doctors! Petticoat surgeons! I'd turn up my toes and die any day before I let a woman try out her doctoring on me."

Only the thought of the wild pony cantering freely in the fields kept me from losing heart. It was as if I lived in two places, at Stagsway and far away at Tumaini. I said nothing more of attending university to Grandfather, for I didn't want to worry him. He was growing weaker. I found him more often in his bed than in his chair. Though I did all I could to interest him in the discoveries I made on my walks, I would look up to find he had dozed off. Only his interest in *Hylocichla guttata pritchardi* remained. For Grandfather the world burned with a small flickering flame, but *Hylocichla guttata pritchardi* burned with a bright fire. My notebook listed three occasions on which I had seen the bird during the summer: first in Mrs. Nessel's herb garden, again in the boxwood maze, and then pecking at a blackberry. Each time Grandfather would ask, "There was no eye ring?"

I would assure him there was not. "There can be no doubt," he said, and sent off another letter to Mr. Pernick.

When autumn came, I returned to school. I was sorry to leave Grandfather, but now I had a goal. I resolved to do the best I could at school. I took physical science and chemistry. When the time came, I would be ready for medical school.

In my last year at Ditchley Nora played Katherina in the school production of *The Taming of the Shrew* and urged me to try out for the part of Bianca. Since the cast practiced the play for hours and hours, we got to know one another, and by the time we put on the play, I found I had close friends. I did well in my exams, and early in the spring of my final year Miss Ethelward asked, "To what university will you go, Rachel?"

On my last visit to Stagsway, I had seen that even lifting a cup of tea was a great effort for Grandfather. "My grandfather isn't well," I said. "I don't see how I can leave him."

"What! Give up your education?"

But I had already made up my mind. I had years ahead of me. I was determined to be a doctor, and if I didn't go to university this year, there would be another year. I tried not to be bitter when the other girls sat for scholarships and were accepted at universities. On the last day of school I received prizes in physical science as well as literature. Frieda was there and tried to persuade me to go on to medical school, but nothing she could say would change my mind. I owed so much to Grandfather, I could not leave him when he most needed me. I had my goal, and now I had only to wait.

It was a sad summer and a sadder autumn and winter. I was reluctant to leave Grandfather for more than a few minutes. Often he slept the day away; sometimes he seemed not to recognize me. Even the magic words *Hylocichla guttata pritchardi* would not rouse him, but still I sent my notes of sightings of the little thrush on to the society.

I spent my days curled up in a chair in Grandfather's room, a book in my hands to pass away the hours. I was reading Virgil. *"Durate, et vosmet rebus servate secondis,"* he wrote. "Endure for a while, and live for a happier day."

When Grandfather was awake, he would ask me to tell him stories of Tumaini. It was a bittersweet time, for I longed to speak of all the things I loved, our little house with the rain beating on our metal roof, visiting the Kikuyu *shamba*s, calming the fears of the mothers when they brought their children in to be inoculated, the thrill of hearing the roar of a lion at night when I was safe inside our house. All the while I was describing my life at Tumaini, I longed for the day to come when I would return as a doctor and there would be a hospital once again.

Perhaps he guessed, for one day when he was more alert than usual, he said, "I think, Rachel, you will not be happy until you have returned to Tumaini."

I did not think it was a time for anything but the truth. "Right now I only want to be here with you, but I do want to return to Africa."

"And will you spend your time there looking at birds?"

"Would you hate it very much if I went to Tumaini as a doctor?"

Grandfather's eyebrows flew up. After a moment he gave me a weak smile. "If I know my Rachel, she will do what she wants to do. And perhaps that is best."

So at last I had no secrets from Grandfather.

It was an April morning, Saint George's day, when Grandfather died. He opened his eyes and tried to sit up in bed. "I can hear my thrush, my *Hylocichla guttata pritchardi*," he said, and then he quoted his favorite poet, Robert Burns: "'Sing on, sweet thrush, upon the leafless bough.'" There was a dreadful strangling sound in his throat. He fell back onto the pillow. A moment later he was gone.

A fog, so thick it felt as if you were looking at the world through gauze curtains, lay over the countryside. All of Stagsway had disappeared into the fog. I couldn't find my bearings. Everything I had depended upon had suddenly vanished. I remember Mrs. Bittery and me comforting each other. I remember Burker bringing in hot tea, his hands shaking so that the cups and saucers danced upon the tray. I called Mr. Grumbloch, and he and Frieda came at once. The house was cold, for the servants were so upset no one had thought to lay fires. Frieda set about with kindling and matches and logs. When she learned I had not had anything to eat all day, she sent Arthur to the kitchen for sandwiches. Mr. Grumbloch made arrangements for Grandfather's funeral.

"He left instructions, you know," Mr. Grumbloch said. "He wants to be buried among the beech trees, just where the land rises."

A notice of Grandfather's death was printed in the London *Times*, and the next day Mr. Pernick hurried down from London. "The moment I heard, I went at once to the society with a request to recognize your grandfather's discovery. You will be pleased," he said, "to find your careful notes substantiated your grandfather's sightings and made the difference. We voted. *Hylocichla guttata pritchardi* is quite official now. It will go down in the books." Mr. Pernick was kindness itself and assured me that there would always be a room kept specially for me at Stagsway.

"You must think of Stagsway as your home," he said. "We are moving the society headquarters here from London, and of course I will be in residence. Anything that can be done to make you comfortable will be done." He gave me a rather coy smile and added, "It would give me so much pleasure to have you here in Stagsway."

There was another call. The Pritchards had seen the notice of Grandfather's death as well. Mr. Grumbloch had not wanted them. "They will be provided for. Surely that is enough. There is no need to inflict them upon us."

But I pleaded that they be allowed to come to the funeral. I could imagine how I would have felt if I had been kept from the funerals of my parents. They came dressed in the darkest black and stood silently in the back of the church like two rooks. When the service was over, they turned quickly and hurried away. I never saw them again.

That spring and summer passed as if the fog had never lifted. My memory of those months is vague. I woke in the morning and went to bed at night. My days were taken up with all the details of turning Stagsway over to the Royal

Bird Society. Mr. Duggen, Mrs. Bittery, Arthur, and Ellie were all to stay on to see to the house for the Society. Grandfather had provided for the rest of the servants and had willed Burker and Mrs. Nessel enough money to retire comfortably. Grandfather had left me money, as well, a great deal of money; some of it I had the use of, the rest I would receive in three years when I turned twenty-one.

"And what will you do now?" Frieda asked. It was late August. The last flowers of autumn were blooming. The fields were orange with hawkweed and lavender with knapweed.

"At the end Grandfather knew I wished to be a doctor. Now there is nothing to stop me."

One morning, without saying a word to anyone, I asked Nivers to drive me into London, and I went at once to the mission society. I had pictured the society as a gloomy place governed by serious and stern men and women, but it was very different than I had imagined.

Miss Lothrop, the director, greeted me warmly. She was tall, six feet if she was an inch, and generously built; she would have been intimidating but for her wide smile and girlish clothes, ruffles and bows everywhere.

"So you are Rachel Sheridan! Let me correct myself, for we have had correspondence with Mr. Grumbloch and of course we talked with Miss Grumbloch. You are Rachel Pritchard now. You were very fortunate to have fallen among such good and generous people. Rachel, how we admired your dear mother and father. What a fine doctor your father was, and what a splendid teacher your mother was. Let people say what they will of orphanages, but then let them hear the story of your parents. We were all saddened by their deaths. It was a great disappointment to have to close Tumaini."

"I came to see if there is a possibility of opening the hospital again."

"Unfortunately, no. I explained it all to your friend Miss Grumbloch. These are difficult times. Money is scarce, and committed as we are to India and China, we are stretched very thin. I'm afraid we have no doctor to send." Miss Lothrop tidied a bow that had come undone.

"What if someone trained as a doctor and then agreed to go to Tumaini?"

"Training takes time and money. We have the time, but we don't have the money to train anyone."

"I have enough money to pay for the education of someone who wishes to become a doctor and who would willingly go to Tumaini. When I am twenty-one, I'll have the money to reopen Tumaini."

Miss Lothrop stared at me. "Well, that is very handsome of you." I could tell from the uncertainty in her voice that she could not quite believe me.

"I'll have Mr. Grumbloch write to you," I said.

At Mr. Grumbloch's name she brightened. "Well, the society will certainly welcome so generous a gift. But who is this candidate who is to become a doctor?"

"It's a young woman, though it might be some time before she is ready."

Miss Lothrop looked shocked. "A young woman? Oh, I hardly think that would be suitable. Even if the mission could reconcile itself to sending a woman doctor, which I doubt, she would have no idea of the rigors of running a hospital in Africa."

I remembered Nora's advice, "give as good as you get," and took a deep breath. "I hope you will have no trouble accepting a woman physician, for if you do, I could not give you the money for the opening of Tumaini."

Miss Lothrop stared at me. "I am not used to having a young girl order the mission about."

"I have no wish to order the mission about. I only want to return to Tumaini and open the hospital. I am going to be a doctor."

THIRTEEN

*I*n the autumn of my eighteenth year I walked through the doors of the London School of Medicine for Women. I thought of my father and all he had known, and all the decisions over life and death he had made. I only hoped I would not disappoint him. The school was on Hunter Street, but we students lived in quarters on Handel Street, where we had our own rooms. The Royal Free Hospital where we trained was nearby on Gray's Inn Road. Years before, the hospital had taken the revolutionary step of opening its doors to women studying to become doctors, the only hospital in London to do so. The hospital, which had started out as barracks for the Light Horse Volunteers, had an imposing entrance on which was carved the British lion. I felt sure the lion was a good omen.

Every time I went to Gray's Inn Road, I thought of the

day I had escaped the Pritchards to seek out Mr. Grumbloch there and at last to tell him the truth. How little I had guessed that one day I would be reading medicine on that very road.

My first lecture each morning was anatomy. Our anatomy textbook was nearly too heavy to hold. I was amazed at the body's many parts. Miss Brose made us memorize all the bits and pieces until I wished we had just been simple amoebas with only a bit of squish to us. Not only did we have to name all the bones of the hand, but she made us put them in a bag and then name them by their feel: lunate, scaphoid, trapezium, capitate, pisiform, and hamate.

Our instructor was as dry as a paragraph in a text, and we imagined her life had been nothing but hospital, classroom, and a small apartment where she kept a cat. Then one day we began to mutter complaints over a long assignment.

Miss Brose heard us. "Sit down this minute and be quiet." We looked at one another, not sure of what was coming. She glared at us and then in a stern voice said, "In 1914 there was a war going on. While you were children, lolling about in gardens and eating your teas, I, along with other women doctors, was sent to the Balkans to care for the Serbian army. We were taking the place of Serbian doctors who had died of typhus because they had to work in filthy hospitals with no beds, no toilets, no food, no water, and no medicine. I walked through open cesspools to get to my patients. The soldiers we treated were covered with lice, and we had to crowd them two to a bed. We were lucky to get three or four hours of sleep at night. Now, would one of you kindly tell me of what you are complaining."

Our teachers pushed us relentlessly. They knew from their own experience that when the time came to qualify for our degree, as women we would find it especially difficult. There was a strong bond among us students. We were quick to help one another. The student who was good in chemistry helped the student who was not. We shared our crushes on young doctors at the Royal Hospital and our broken hearts when they ignored us. We took one another's blood pressure, listened to one another's hearts, and practiced drawing blood on one another. When we were faced with our first cadaver, smelling partly of formaldehyde and stinking partly of rot, because it had not been well preserved, we all held our noses and plunged in, covering for the students who were in the lavatory throwing up. When we all stood on the balcony of the operating room to watch our first operation, and a bloody one it was, there was the comfort of being together.

I seemed to be in charge of death. I was the only one who had faced death often and learned to accept it and see beyond it. It was not only the deaths of my parents but all my years at Tumaini, when patients we knew and cared for deeply would die in spite of all we could do for them. Most of the other students were seeing death for the first time. If it was a patient they had cared for, they blamed themselves. I consoled them, reminding them of all the patients they had helped. I told them doctors were not miracle workers, but when a little girl in my ward died of meningitis, only the severe look of the attending doctor made me fight back my own tears.

We seldom had any leisure. Our days were filled with classes and laboratories and our nights with study. Some of the students joined the choral society and the hardier ones crewed on the rowing eight. In our third year, when we became clerks, we were on the hospital wards twenty hours at a time. On those few days when I had an hour or two, I walked over to the British Museum, which was close by. I wandered through the ancient Greek and Egyptian galleries, but my favorite spot was the manuscript room, with letters written by the kings and queens of England, Henry VIII and poor Anne Boleyn, and Queen Elizabeth and Queen Victoria. There was a description of the execution of Queen Mary Stuart, and you could see Napoleon's signature. The most romantic thing was a letter Lord Nelson had started to his mistress, Lady Hamilton, just before the battle of Trafalgar. I thought that room better than a dozen history books.

On Sundays I went to services at the nearby foundling hospital, which wasn't a hospital at all but an orphanage for children of mothers unable to care for their babies. There were nearly five hundred children, all dressed in the hospital's quaint costumes. When the mothers left their children, they often left a memento for the child: a lock of the mother's hair, an earring, or a lace glove. It would be all the child would have to remember his mother. Always as I listened to the children singing like angels, I would hope that my own mother was looking down and rejoicing that I had escaped an orphanage and found so kind a man to care for me. And I hoped that the kind man, my grandfather, was pleased that I was going to be a doctor.

One Sunday afternoon I followed the crowds to the zoological gardens in Regent's Park. As I wandered through the aviary, where birds I had seen flying about freely in Tumaini were shut into cages, I had gloomy thoughts about how I was imprisoned in London and in school. From a distance I heard a sound I had not heard since I had come to England. People must have thought I had lost my mind, for I stood absolutely still, my eyes wide, my mouth open. Lions. I followed the signs to the lion house and stood there staring at the ragged lions pacing back and forth, feeling as strong a passion as they did to escape my imprisonment in the city and return to my home. For a wild moment I thought of unlocking their cages. For weeks I dreamed of the lions. Sometimes they were imprisoned in their cages, and I would awake breathless and shaking, and sometimes they were free and wandering in the bush, and I would sleep on peacefully. I never went back to the zoo.

The school was near to Gray's Inn, and once or twice a term Mr. Grumbloch gave me lunch at Simpson's, where the waiters would roll out a cart on which lay a huge roast of beef. Mr. Grumbloch would inquire of me just what cut and degree of rareness I wished, and then would relay my wishes to the waiter as if the waiter had not heard me. Our meals at school were meager and taken on the run, so I ate every bit of the beef, and afterward a slice of apple tart with a great hunk of Stilton cheese.

Mr. Grumbloch would gravely tell me how my shares and bonds were doing and assure me that financially I was what he always referred to as "comfortable," which made me imagine that the bank was filled with pound notes sewn into soft cushions and comforters.

At first I spent my vacations at Stagsway. Mr. Pernick had kept his promise to put aside a room for me, but now it no longer seemed my home. In my mind and in my heart I was already living in Tumaini. Enthusiastic bird lovers from all over the world had taken over Stagsway. They were out in every kind of weather sloshing about in rubber boots, binoculars strung around their necks. We all sat at a common table for meals, and I listened to them recite to one another the list of birds they had seen that day. Everyone hoped to find the *Hylocichla guttata pritchardi*, and in the rare event one was spotted, it was an occasion of great celebration and Grandfather was toasted. I would have been happy to continue my vacations at Stagsway, but on a summer afternoon after my second year Mr. Pernick asked if he might join me for a walk in the New Forest, where I had long ago found the wild pony. Mr. Pernick had lately made me nervous with his kindnesses. He was forever opening doors for me, bringing me cups of tea, and complimenting my dullest dresses.

It was a lovely summer day, and uncharitably I wished that I were able to enjoy the birdsong and the flowers without Mr. Pernick pausing to draw my attention to the birds and the blooms as if I could not see them for myself. When we were well away from the house, Mr. Pernick paused, and I thought he had come upon some bird he wanted to study. I waited for him to raise his binoculars. Instead, after clearing his throat several times, he said, "I wonder, Miss Pritchard, if you have given any thought to your future."

"Yes, Mr. Pernick. You know I plan to go back to Tumaini."

"Very commendable, but I was thinking of your *personal* future."

One look at his red face and trembling lower lip and I knew at once what he was about to say. For a desperate second I considered fleeing into the forest and hiding. Anxious to head him off, I quickly said, "Mr. Pernick, I am so busy with my studies, I haven't any time for thoughts of a personal nature."

"I would never discourage you from your dream, Miss Pritchard. For myself, if I could have you for a companion, it would be the achievement of a lifetime to be able to study and live among the birds of Africa."

There was no place in my dream of Tumaini for Mr. Pernick, and I told him so in the kindest words I could.

After that I spent my vacations with Frieda on Gordon Square. Frieda took me to the theater and the ballet and made me spend money on clothes. She had given up her sweeping skirts for skirts that showed her knees. Her long hair was cut in a bob. There were always people about talking of artists I had never heard of, Pablo Picasso and Joan Miró, and books I had no time to read, T. E. Lawrence's *Seven Pillars of Wisdom*, and *Mrs. Dalloway*, by someone called Virginia Woolf, who came once to Frieda's. Virginia Woolf had wonderful hooded eyes and whispered to me unkind and funny things about all the other guests.

There were intense arguments about the Russian revolution and a political party in Germany called the National Socialist German Workers' Party. Frieda's friends were as exotic to me as the bird lovers had been. They were all brilliant. They wrote books and painted pictures, and if they ever stopped talking, which I was sure they would never do, they planned to change the world. I would sit in a corner and listen to them by the hour, and then I would go up to my room and my own books with their pictures of bones and muscles, their charts that told how many with a disease might live and how many might die, for I knew it was those books that would lead me back to Tumaini.

Our senior year we all waited to see in which hospital we would do our residencies. With the exception of the Royal Free Hospital, which had long had a close relationship with our school and where we had done our clerking, most of the hospitals were closed to women. During the war, when medical students were scarce, the hospitals reluctantly threw open their doors. Now many of those doors were once again shut. St. George's and St. Mary's hospitals had already gone back to refusing women. I hoped for the Royal Free Hospital, where I had been so happy in my work, but when I received my assignment, I saw that I was going to be at Westminster Hospital. A woman from India, Janaki Kumar, who had been in my class, was also assigned to Westminster. I didn't know Janaki well. She was older than most of us and kept to herself. Now I told her, "I'm going to ask Miss Brose if she can get me transferred to the Royal Free Hospital. There's already talk that the Westminster wants to get rid of women residents. Do you want me to put in a word for you?"

"No, no. I will go where I am sent. It is all the same to

me, and I hear very good things about the quality of medicine at Westminster."

When I tackled Miss Brose, she only smiled. "We mean you no harm, Rachel. We know exactly what you and Janaki are in for. It was our belief that of all the girls, you two could survive the difficulties. We have all had to be pioneers. When I was at training, I was made to go out of the room when a man was examined below the navel. I persevered. I expect you to do the same."

Even the location of the hospital was intimidating, close as it was to the great Westminster Abbey and the Houses of Parliament. Janaki and I were the only women among thirty residents. At first we were accepted, for the male residents, like ourselves, were all dreading hospital rounds with the chief of medicine, Dr. Raspton, who was rumored to have a vile temper. We all stood huddled together like a miserable clutch of pullets waiting to be pecked at by the rooster. Dr. Raspton was tall and thin, like a statue whose every spare ounce of clay had been carved away by the sculptor. He had thin pitiless lips, eyes like a hawk's, and an arrogant manner.

At once he singled Janaki and me out. "Ah, Miss Pritchard and Miss Kumar, what a pleasure to have two young ladies with us to temper our rudeness. I suppose we can count on you for a few months? No marriage in sight as yet to take you away from a career in medicine, as happens to most women doctors?" The male residents snickered, glad not to be a target of Raspton's satire.

"No, Sir," Janaki said, but I was foolish, and knowing that a common objection to women in medicine was that they would be trained and then leave the profession to marry, I said, "A study has just been done, Sir, of women who have graduated from the London School of Medicine for Women, and the study showed that only two or three of the hundreds of graduates are not practicing."

There was absolute silence. I realized at once what I had done. Dr. Raspton glared at me. "I was under the impression that I was to be the teacher," he said, "but I see that it is not to be. Miss Pritchard, suppose you lead the rounds."

I was trembling so I could hardly open my mouth. "I'm very sorry, Dr. Raspton. I didn't mean to talk out of turn."

"Well, let us carry on." He gave Janaki and me a cunning look. "We don't want to injure your sensibilities, young women, so if there is anything that you find difficult or embarrassing, you will let us know?"

"Yes, Sir," we said. My face was burning, but Janaki appeared unconcerned.

The last patient on the rounds was a man with jaundice. There could be no question, for he was as yellow as a lemon. The patient's record was passed around among us students. "Well, Osborn"—Dr. Raspton chose a young resident who looked stunned at being singled out—"give us your diagnosis."

Mr. Osborn studied the patient's record. Stuttering with fear, he replied, "I would say it was the man's liver."

"Would you indeed?" Dr. Raspton looked at the rest of us. "And is there another opinion?"

From the records I saw the man had chills and fever, headache and nausea. I had seen similar symptoms at Tumaini in patients suffering from the bites of certain kinds of lice. I think I believed I could get back in Dr. Raspton's good graces by answering his question. Of course I should have known better. "Could it be the bite of some insect, Sir?" I asked. "Perhaps a louse?"

Dr. Raspton's hawk's eyes narrowed. He had his prey in sight. "Well, well, Miss Pritchard, you have managed to make your fellow residents look especially foolish this morning. You are correct, though not quite correct. If you were in Africa, you might find these symptoms caused by lice. In England it is caused by ticks. I hope the men in the class will feel free to come to you for help, since by comparison with you, they appear to be quite stupid."

I felt twenty-eight pairs of furious eyes trained on me. After that, any task that might be considered remotely embarrassing to a young woman was left to me by the male residents. Janaki was sympathetic. "But Rachel," she said, "you needn't have told everything you knew right at the beginning."

Not all the doctors were hostile to women. When at the end of the year one of the residents, Edgar Nealthingham, asked the neurologist if it wasn't true that women's brains were smaller than men's, the doctor said, "Yes, Mr. Nealthingham, it is quite true and certainly a puzzle, since Miss Pritchard and Miss Kumar got first-class honors in their London examinations this year while you barely scraped through."

The residents would give one another sly looks when I had to complete examinations on male patients, but there was nothing that I had not seen long before at Tumaini. When I had first begun to work in the hospital, my father had said, "God fashioned the human body, Rachel. Every bit of it is God's work, so there is no need for shame."

Janaki was never bothered by the residents' superior attitude.

"Don't they make you angry?" I asked, for I would cheerfully have choked them all.

"It doesn't matter to me, Rachel. I have been sent here to learn the newest medicines and techniques and to take them back with me to India. A wealthy family in India is paying for my education here, and it is a great expense for them. There is no need for me to waste my time in useless anger. I have only to think of the women in India who need my help. Until there were women doctors, Indian women in purdah—that is, women who were not allowed to go out in public or to have anything to do with a man outside of their family—could not go to a doctor. No matter how ill they were, their sickness could only be described to another person, who would then describe it to a doctor. The doctor would make a diagnosis, but he would never be allowed to see the patient. Think of a woman dying an agonizing death because no male doctor could touch her. No, let them make fun of us. They are nothing to me."

Shamed, after that I kept my head down and my mouth shut. By our last year the early antagonisms were forgotten. We were all comrades. We had been through so much together, we were like people in a lifeboat upon a raging sea. All we cared about was our survival. On the day that I qualified as a physician, and my name was written down on the register, I went to the mission board. I was twenty-three and had received my inheritance. I had already sent a check to the board for the supplies I would need in Tumaini. Now I proudly went there to show off my physician's license.

Miss Lothrop, with as many bows and ruffles as ever, congratulated me. There was none of the doubt she had shown before. I don't think she would have chosen a woman doctor for the mission, but now that one was available, I think she was resigned. In an indifferent voice she said, "We are very pleased." And then she smiled at me and said, "How proud your father would be."

FOURTEEN

I made a last trip to Stagsway. Over the years it had changed. There was less of Grandfather there and more of the Royal Bird Society.

Mr. Duggen complained. "They tramp right through my roses to see the birds what don't get close enough for them. I believe they'd like 'em served up on a silver platter."

Still, I knew Grandfather would be pleased to see how enthusiastic his visitors were and how, in spite of Mr. Duggen's abused roses, Stagsway kept its charm. Ellie and Arthur had married, and Mr. Pernick shyly confided, "I'm pleased to say I'm engaged, Miss Pritchard, to a charming woman who is particularly knowledgeable about the migrating habits of the *Motacilla trochilus*."

Though he made no effort to stop me, Mr. Grumbloch was astounded that I wished to go back to Tumaini. "You are leaving civilization for heat and dust and wild animals. I don't see it."

Frieda was delighted. She had very odd ideas of what was worn in Africa and took me to Liberty on Regent Street to buy silk frocks, "for garden parties," and to Brigg in St. James's Street to buy umbrellas and parasols, "to keep the sun from your complexion."

"I'll never have an occasion for a silk dress," I pleaded, "and a straw hat will take care of my complexion."

The Grumblochs saw me off, Mr. Grumbloch furnishing me with money orders and Keating's insect powder and Frieda with Cadbury chocolates and Virginia Woolf's latest novel. Frieda promised to visit me. "I want to see if Tumaini really exists."

I thought the four-week voyage would never end. So eager was I to reach Africa that at times the ship seemed caught in the water like a leaf endlessly turning around in a pool. I ate my chocolates, read my books, dined, and chatted with the other passengers, but my mind was always sailing ahead of the ship. Would I be able to rebuild Tumaini? Would the lives of the Kikuyu and Masai be safe in my hands? Would the Kikuyu and Masai trust me? One day I answered the questions one way and the next day another way. I was like the leopard at the moment before it springs, tasting only what was to come.

We suffered through a terrible storm with rolling seas. We saw flying fish and dolphins follow the ship like obedient puppies. We had singsongs after dinner, and there were masquerade balls and tea dances. There were charades and games of bridge and backgammon and shuffleboard tournaments and badminton contests. There were flirtations and quarrels and visits to ports. This time I saw Alexandria, but mostly I was bored and impatient, so that finally, when Mombasa's ancient fort came into view, I wept with relief.

The train from Mombasa to Nairobi chugged along slowly, but now I didn't care, for on either side of the railway were the familiar tall grasses and flat-topped acacia trees, and in the distance my old friend, Mount Kenya. Medicines and surgical equipment were waiting for me in Nairobi, and so was my automobile, a Ford truck that I could use to carry supplies to Tumaini. The gentleman at the garage where I picked up the truck was obviously surprised to see that R. Pritchard was a young woman; however, the car had been paid for and he turned it over to me. He pointed out the superior gear shift, the double-beam headlights, and the hand-operated windshield wipers and then waited for me to drive off.

When I stood there for some minutes, he asked, "Is there some difficulty with the truck, Madam?"

With a scarlet face, I murmured, "I've never driven an automobile."

"Ah," he said. "Perhaps I might just demonstrate the basic workings of it for you." More uncertainly he added,

"And then I could accompany you while you gave the truck a little run about the city."

So began what must have been the most terrifying moments of the gentleman's life, but after a bit I caught on, and leaving him at the garage, I collected all my equipment and a large cat, for I had not forgotten the rats that had wandered into our house. The cat was the tawny color of a lion, and for a name I gave it the Swahili word for lion, Simba. Full of joy, I drove to Tumaini, stirring up a plume of red dust like the veil of a bride on her way to the happiest day of her life.

Time in Africa is not like time in England, where an ancient ruin stands stone on stone for the centuries. Man is not the master in Africa. As I turned off the main road from Nairobi onto the road that led to Tumaini, a road that I had known well, I hesitated. It was no longer a road, but an overgrown track, a trail that might have been made by animals traveling to and from a waterhole.

Seeing what even a few short years had done, I had my first doubts. With the grasses sweeping the bottom of the truck, I pushed on, afraid that any minute it would plunge into an antbear hole or get stuck in soft sand. When at last I reached Tumaini, just as I feared, Tumaini wasn't there.

The rains had dissolved the mud bricks. The *bati*, the corrugated iron of the roof, had been carried away to become someone else's roof or perhaps to make bracelets. Ants had made a meal of the wooden doors. If someone dies in a Kikuyu hut, the Kikuyu think it unlucky and burn down the hut. It was like that with Tumaini. There had been deaths, and now everything had moldered away. After my initial shock I scoured the grasses, determined to find some evidence that Tumaini had existed, but the only proof I found were the crosses that marked my parents' graves and the graves of Kanoro's father and the missionary. And Valerie's grave. Someone was tending the small graveyard.

As I stood there telling my parents that I had returned and what I meant to do, I noticed a movement among the bushes. I was ready to run back to the truck when Kanoro stepped out. Or I thought it was Kanoro, the Kanoro whom I recalled from my childhood.

"*Bibi* Rachel?" He backed away from me as if I were a spirit, and no telling whether good or evil.

"Kanoro?"

"*Nina itwa Ngigi.*"

Nina itwa: "I am called." The first Swahili words I had heard since leaving Tumaini. Of course, years had passed. It was Kanoro's son, Ngigi, the *mtoto* whose leg I had nursed. I saw that around his neck was a cord and strung onto the cord a small black-and-silver ornament. A part of a stethoscope! That remnant of Tumaini gave me hope. Swahili words came back to me in a rush. "Ngigi, you are a young man."

"Yes, and I have a wife and a bit of land and soon a child. Are you truly here?"

"Oh, yes. I've come to stay. I mean to open the hospital again. Will you help me, Ngigi? And tell me where your *baba* is and Ita and Wanja and Nduta and everyone from the hospital."

He seemed surprised that I did not know these things. He explained as if to a small child, "They are all at their *shamba*s except Nduta, who has gone to live with her husband's family. My *baba* is at his *shamba* also, but he shivers and sweats and does not stir about much. If you bring back the hospital, will a doctor come to make him well?"

"Ngigi, I am a doctor now. I'll come and see your *baba* at once." Ngigi did not seem in the least surprised to find I was a doctor, and I remembered that there were women witch doctors as well as men. At least here I would have no battle to fight.

I took up my medicine bag and followed Ngigi, learning as I hurried along the familiar path that Ngigi came regularly to keep the graveyard from disappearing into the bush. "*Baba* sends me," Ngigi said. "You gave a promise to him to return, and he would not have you find the graves of your parents gone to nothing. For us a grave means little, but with you it is different." The Kikuyu carried their dead into the fields, and the insects and the vultures cleaned the bones. It was not unusual to find a bleached bone or even a skull. I thought it would not be a bad thing to end your days scraped clean and resting in the sun.

I all but ran to Kanoro's *shamba*. He had aged. When I threw my arms around him, it was like embracing the small bones of a sparrow.

"*Nzuri! Nzuri!*" Kanoro said, and I thought how there is no word in English that means both wonderful and terrible and yet at this moment it was the perfect word, for it was wonderful to be back and to have my arms around Kanoro and it was terrible that Tumaini had disappeared and Kanoro was so ill.

"Now, tell me of your sickness," I said. When I examined him, I found Kanoro was suffering from a severe bout of malaria. Relieved that it was something I could treat, I gave him medicine and ordered rest.

With all of Kanoro's family about, I was escorted to the one bench in the hut. "Let us hear your story," Kanoro said. They were amazed at my long journey across the ocean to the land where snow fell. "The house I lived in," I said, "had enough rooms for a whole Kikuyu village." They did not quite believe what I told them, but they enjoyed the hearing of it. At last they wanted to know of my plans for the hospital.

"We must find many people to make bricks," I said, "and we will have to dig a new well, a large one, and we must do it quickly, for the cots have been ordered and the laboratory equipment and a generator as large as your hut. This time the hospital will have all it needs, Kanoro. Now you must get well so that you can help me. I'll be back tomorrow," I promised.

Ngigi stood in front of me as I started to leave. "You will need someone at your side," he said. "Until my *baba* is well, let me be that person."

I was grateful to Ngigi. Even as a child I had known that though we imagined ourselves in charge, the Kikuyu understood very well that we would perish without them.

Though the evening was cool, I slept in the bed of the truck, Simba curled at my feet. I could smell the smoke from fires set by the Masai to burn off grass for planting. A male and female spotted owl courted one another. A toad shrilled. At last, and from a great distance, I heard the sound for which I had been hungering, the low roar of a lion. When I fell asleep, it was to the sounds that had been my lullaby as a child.

In the morning Ngigi awoke me. He had brought a dozen men. By afternoon I had a mud-walled house with a thatched roof and a line of people, some of them ill and some who merely said that they were ill so that they might see the red-haired witch doctor. Once I had to leave the line of patients to hide in the cab of the truck and cry, for I was where I wanted to be and doing what I had dreamed of doing.

The next day I was up at dawn. I waited impatiently for the men to return so that we could begin work on the foundation of the hospital, but though I waited until noon, no men came and Ngigi would not explain their absence, though I was sure he understood the reason. Just as I was ready to go to Kanoro's *shamba* and ask his advice, Ngigi came to me with a worried frown puckering his young face. "*Bibi* Rachel, Wangombe comes."

"Who is Wangombe?" From the fear in Ngigi's voice, I knew it must be someone bringing trouble with him.

"The old chief of your father's time, Mabui, is dead, and Wangombe is chief now. He is a man who is a chief at all times, even when he eats and sleeps."

Wangombe appeared with a small retinue of followers. He was splendid in strings of shells and beads, a cloak of monkey fur, and a headdress of ostrich plumes. I stood up and greeted him formally, bowing. He did the same, and we faced each other warily, waiting to see who would speak the first word. At last I said, "Wangombe, I am honored to see you here."

"*Msabu*, you would not come to me, so I have come to you."

I saw at once what my mistake had been and was furious with myself, for I knew better. I was in Wangombe's territory. Wangombe's men had worked all day for me. All this without my consulting with Wangombe. "Wangombe, I have been away from this land for many years and in the land of another chief." When I saw his face cloud, I hastened to add, "One not so great as you. Because that other chief was not so great, I had forgotten the power of a chief and his importance. I see my mistake. You were very generous to allow your men to come here yesterday. I have many, many days' work ahead. I hope you will allow your men to help me."

"I would be honored to have my men give help, but there is the matter of their crops. The planting must be done and the crops cared for. They cannot be spared."

It was the women who planted the crops and tended them. The men would have nothing to do with crops. "Wangombe, I know it will be a great sacrifice for the men to give up the tending of the crops. You will tell me what a suitable wage is for such a sacrifice."

After that there was heavy bargaining, with Ngigi whispering in my ear that Wangombe was asking too much. At last we came to an agreement, and as if by magic the men appeared and cheerfully went to work.

I had been making plans for the hospital for years, but I had been young when the hospital had been there, and I didn't know what its problems had been. Ita and Wanja and Jata were found. We all sat together at Kanoro's *shamba*, and I drew pictures with a sharp stick on the packed dirt floor of Kanoro's hut. Jata was as bossy as ever, but her ideas were useful. "There must be space in the children's room for the mothers to sleep." And I agreed, for I remembered many a mother who would not leave her child at night and slept under the child's cot.

Ita was a great help, for he had worked in the operating room. "We must have doors that close firmly, *Bibi*

Rachel, so that the relatives don't gather to look over our shoulders."

Kanoro said, "There must be a place without trees or dried grasses for the families to cook their *posho* and roast their goats without setting fires."

Chief Wangombe came often and had his own suggestions. He had once been to Nairobi and had seen the three-story hotel. "One house sits on another house," he said, "and on that other house yet one more house. The putting of houses on top of one another would save more land for growing crops or for pasture."

I grew fond of Ngigi. He was more solemn than his father and thought of things beyond the *shamba*s and villages. He confided to me, "A Kikuyu from Nairobi visited the *shamba*s and spoke of 'Africa for the Africans.' He told of a leader called Jomo Kenyatta. My father ordered the man to go away, but I followed him and listened. The government gave land to the English soldiers who fought in the war. Some of that land had been farmed by the Kikuyu. The government gave no land to the Kikuyu who went to war for them. That is not fair. The Kikuyu are not allowed to own land. Why is that? The man, Kenyatta, spoke of *uhuru*. Was I wrong to listen?"

The word *uhuru* means freedom, a word dear to me. "I don't think you were wrong to listen," I told Ngigi.

Not only patients came, but peddlers arrived at my doorway with eggs and chickens, squash, bananas, and even goats and sheep. I had been gathered in by the people.

I had ordered a small piano, and on Sundays there were church services again. Kanoro, who was much better, came with his family and sang in a loud, sure voice, for he had not forgotten the hymns.

I had one sad duty. I wrote to Mr. Grumbloch to contact the Pritchards about Valerie's grave. An answer came. The Pritchards wished to have Valerie's coffin returned to England. At last Valerie left the country she so disliked, and I thought of the pony I had seen galloping happily through the grasses and wildflowers of the New Forest.

While waiting for the operating room to be finished and the delivery of a generator to give us electricity, I could attempt little surgery. Instead I treated the lepers, the infections, and the fevers, and brought babies into the world when they were stubborn about coming. By day I was overwhelmed by *wasiwasi*: a crooked wall, men who did not show up for work, constant trips into Nairobi to bring back supplies in the little truck.

In the evening when the last patient left and Ngigi went home, I counted the new rows of brick that had been laid that day at the hospital and ate a supper of cold chicken and beans. I sat on my porch looking out at the way the hills leaned against the horizon, thinking often of Mother and Father, sure that they would be pleased with the hospital.

It was February, hot, and too early for the rains. All around me were the rustling sounds of small night creatures, like the light fingers of a child tapping your shoulder for attention. In the distance I could hear the lions, restless in the heat, roaring their complaints. I thought of the lions in the zoo at Regent's Park and mourned for them in their captivity. The little green monkeys bickered with one another in the baobab tree, and the bat-eared foxes that slept by day crept out to hunt for termites. A gecko climbed the mud walls of the house to catch the insects attracted by the hurricane lamp. When I awoke at dawn, it was to the sad calls of the wood doves with pale-pink breasts the color of the sunrise.

I knew there would be *wasiwasi*, troubles that no medicine could cure. Drought might come, and with drought, starvation. The government was raising the hut tax and taking land from the Kikuyu reserves. How long would the Kikuyu put up with that? I could not tell the government what to do or bring the rains. I had dreams for Tumaini, dreams of a large hospital with the latest equipment and many doctors, a school for the children, and a nursing school. Many of my dreams for Tumaini might come to nothing, but Tumaini was the Swahili word for hope.

GLOSSARY

*S*wahili is an African language that incorporates words from a number of different languages, including Arabic and English. It is pronounced just as it is written.

baba: father
bati: corrugated iron
bibi: miss
bwana: mister or master
memsahib: mistress; pronounced *msabu* by some
mtoto: child
mzimu: dead person
ngoma: a ceremonial dance
nina itwa: I am called
nozuri: wondrous
panga: a broad-bladed knife
popo: bat
posho: maize porridge
shamba: farm
sobai (Masai): good morning
tumaini: hope
uhuru: freedom
wasiwasi: worries, troubles

AUTHOR'S NOTE

*L*istening for Lions is a work of fiction, but I am especially indebted to Dr. C. Albert Snyder for sharing reminiscences of his years as a missionary physician in Rwanda, Africa. When Dr. Snyder and his wife, Louise, first went to Kibogora hospital in Rwanda in 1968, it was a 40-bed rural clinic. It is now a 175-bed full-service medical center with two surgeries, outpatient clinics, and a maternity and nursing school. Dr. Snyder retired in 1990, but in April 1993 a surgeon was needed at Kibogora and Dr. Snyder and his wife returned to Rwanda, only to be forced to leave in the wake of the brutal uprising that killed hundreds of thousands of Rwandans. In 1994 he again returned to Kibogora hospital. A journal of those years and of his struggle to be a missionary doctor in the most challenging of circumstances appears in his book, *On a Hill Far Away*.

BIBLIOGRAPHY

The following books were especially helpful:

Amidon, Lynne A. *An Illustrated History of the Royal Free Hospital.* London: The Royal Free Hospital, 1996.

Bell, E. Moberly. *Storming the Citadel: The Rise of the Woman Doctor.* London: Constable & Co. Ltd., 1953.

Dinesen, Isak. *Letters from Africa, 1914–1931.* Chicago: University of Chicago Press, 1981.

Snyder, C. Albert. *On a Hill Far Away: Journal of a Missionary Doctor in Rwanda.* Indianapolis, Ind.: Light and Life Press, 1995.

White, Gilbert. *The Natural History of Selborne.* London: Oxford University Press, 1789.

Zimmerman, Dale A., et al. *Birds of Kenya and Northern Tanzania.* Princeton, N.J.: Princeton University Press, 1996.